UNTAMED INSTINCT

A STEAMY SHIFTER AND WITCH ROMANCE

ALASKA ALPHAS

TAMSIN LEY

AURORA SHIFTERS

Twin Leaf Press

Cover by Tamsin Ley

Paperback version
ISBN-13: 978-1-950027-21-7
Copyright © 2020 Twin Leaf Press
All Rights Reserved.

Twin Leaf Press
PO Box 672255
Chugiak, AK 99567

An outcast from his pack

Born to a family of wolves, mountain lion shifter Adrian Stone has never fit into the shifter community. He's resolved to live out his days alone, prowling the Alaskan wilderness and hunting down rogues. When he rescues a stunning, determined human who smells like catnip and makes his inner animal purr, he's shocked, because his mountain lion insists she's his mate - even though she claims to be a witch...

A witch without magic

Darcy Mae is determined to join her aunt's coven and make up for her mother's mistakes. All she needs is one more ingredient for a potion to cheat the coven's test. But a grizzly attacks her while she's searching for herbs, and her mountain lion rescuer transforms into a man with rock-hard abs and golden eyes she can't resist...

Witches and shifters never mix, and Darcy is terrified the coven will drive her away. But the coven isn't her only concern. The local shifters believe the rogue outbreak is due to witchcraft.

And Darcy is the perfect target.

Reader note: A reclusive shifter, a wanna-be witch, and a

whole lot of hot and steamy purring. Intended for mature audiences.

CHAPTER ONE

Adrian crouched among the cottonwood leaves, claws digging into the bark as he surveyed the dead moose in the clearing below. He'd been waiting here in his mountain lion form for several hours and was eager to move on, but had to be certain the carcass had been deserted before he drew closer to investigate. He'd received numerous reports of abandoned animal kills over the last few weeks, and his supervisor at the ranger station wanted whoever—or whatever—was doing the poaching to be tracked down.

Scattered throughout the Wrangell-St. Elias Park, the previous sites had been old before Adrian reached them, the evidence around the carcasses obscured by smaller predators and decay. This site seemed fresher, the stench of rot less intense, although flies swarmed over the bull's hide and stubby, velvet-covered antlers. If the killer was human, they weren't out for trophies. And they definitely weren't doing it for meat. Someone or something was killing for fun, and they were slowly moving closer to human-occupied lands.

Adrian's tail twitched angrily, and he let out a grunt of resignation before dropping nimbly to the ground. The scent of rotting flesh grew stronger as he approached, and flies rose in a cloud, exposing gashes writhing with fresh maggots.

He circled the moose, estimating it had been dead slightly longer than twenty-four hours. Clawed paw prints, almost twice the size of his own, scarred the earth around the kill. He lowered his muzzle and sniffed, tail lashing. The familiar musk of a grizzly filled his nose. *Shifter grizzly*. He released a hiss of displeasure. The last thing the shifter community wanted was a rogue member drawing attention to the national park. Randall, Adrian's tough-as-nails wolf supervisor, would not like this.

Fuck, Adrian didn't like it either. Mountain lions weren't unheard of in Alaska, but rare enough to cause a ruckus among humans if sighted. The vast wilds of the park were his refuge—his *territory* in the mind of his mountain lion. The local bear shifters would want to take care of a rogue grizzly themselves.

Adrian exposed his canines and turned away, prowling through the trees toward his ranger cabin to call his supervisor.

Just out of sight of his cabin, he shifted and retrieved the uniform he kept in a hollow tree, shrugging into his clothing before emerging into the clearing. His cabin was a small log building nestled next to one of the many rock faces jutting from the mountain, roof covered in thick moss and a small porch screened in from mosquitoes. One of the more popular trailheads started nearby, and a small message board fluttered with notices campers left to each other at the end of his overgrown driveway.

Inside the two-room cabin, a few small windows shed dusky light over the sparse furnishings. Passing the small front area with a table, a propane fridge, a wood stove, and an old sofa, he moved to the bedroom where a king-sized bed took up almost every inch of space. He retrieved his cell phone from the nightstand and moved to the corner of the front room where he got the best reception. He kept an old ham radio in the shed for when the notoriously spotty cell service didn't work, but he couldn't talk to Randall about shifter business over the radio. Thankfully, the phone showed two bars today. He dialed the main ranger office.

"This is HQ," a woman's nasal voice answered.

"Cherry, it's Adrian. I need to talk to Randall."

"Oh, hi, handsome!" Her voice brightened. "We haven't heard from you in a while. How've you been?"

Adrian bared his teeth and reminded himself to be polite; Cherry was human. "Doing fine."

He hated social niceties, which was why he'd become a ranger in the first place. This remote location suited him well, and he only ventured into town when he needed supplies. Most of his duties allowed him to patrol the trails alone, talking to the occasional hiker and reporting any problems. Several times a year he had to oversee search and rescue operations when a hiker got lost, but more often than not, he found the missing person before a full team even arrived.

"You doing okay on handouts?" Cherry chirped back.

He glanced toward the door where a stack of papers had gathered a layer of dust. He was supposed to pass them out to tourists, but since he avoided people, he used very few. "All good. I just need to talk to Randall."

"You betcha."

The phone clicked. A few heartbeats later, the supervisor's voice came on the line. "Adrian, what's up?"

"I've got a lead on the poacher. I found a spike-fork moose abandoned yesterday, and there's fresh grizzly sign all over the place. Smells like a shifter."

"Shit. Don't tell me the infection's moved to our territory."

"What infection?"

"Rogues." The sound of fingernails against beard stubble scratched over the phone line. "Two rogue wolves and a moose were put down in Anchorage over the winter, then a black bear outside Valdez this spring. No rhyme or reason to why. Council sent out a memo a while back. Don't you read your emails, Adrian?"

Adrian glanced at the dust-covered laptop under the nightstand. "Not like I have wifi out here, Randall. I'll catch up next time I go into town."

Randall made a frustrated noise over the phone. "Well, if a shifter's behind these abandoned kills, it's likely a rogue. File your report then go handle it ASAP."

"Me? Isn't this Den business?" Although the Council oversaw shifter law, local shifter groups liked to take care of their own business.

"Not this time. A travel blogger already posted about the kills. We need to get ahead of the news before it goes viral. Take your rifle."

"I'm a ranger, not a SWAT team, Randall."

"This is your territory. I need you to handle it. There could be hikers in danger."

"Fuck." Adrian grimaced. "What if he shifts before he dies?" It was one thing for a ranger to take down a dangerous bear. Quite another if a human body showed up killed by a ranger's bullet. And in a face-to-face fight, a mountain lion couldn't stand up to a full-grown grizzly, especially a shifter gone rogue.

"Make your first shot count."

"I hate this shit." Hanging up, Adrian pocketed his phone and grabbed his rifle before heading back outside. He'd file a report when he got back. Best to get on the trail while it was still relatively warm.

He started up his ATV, its disused engine letting out a disgusting belch of smoke. The damn thing cut off his ability to hear or smell anything, which made his mountain lion bristle in discomfort. *I know, me too.* But he couldn't carry his rifle while in feline form.

Stowing the weapon in the mounted case on the front of the ATV, he rolled out of the cabin's clearing toward the trailhead parking lot.

CHAPTER TWO

 $\mathcal{D}$ arcy stopped her Subaru and eyed the overgrown path. According to Google, this dirt road should lead to a trailhead parking lot, but it looked like if she drove any farther, she might end up "parked" more permanently. Her all-wheel drive had managed the old, rutted road, but the path was getting narrower, with branches rubbing her door panels. *Did I take a wrong turn?*

She glanced in her rearview mirror. There had been a space wide enough to turn around a short way back. Putting the car in reverse, she carefully maneuvered through the brush, backing into a flat area that looked like it would make a nice campsite.

The overcast sky filtered dimly through the thick canopy of trees, and she hadn't seen a soul since turning into what had started out as a fairly decent dirt road. She rolled down her window and breathed in the verdant forest air. *This looks like as good a place to start as any.*

Her interview with the coven was the day after tomorrow, and she'd come in search of herbs to make an eloquence potion. This would be her last-ditch effort to overcome the stutter that ruined every spell she tried to cast. Poor Aunt Willow still had a patch of white hair behind one ear from one of her lessons. Darcy'd tried to buy an eloquence potion from the local apothecary shop, but it turned out it only worked for the person who made it, and the effects would not be permanent. But she didn't need to be *good* at incantations, only steady enough to pass the coven's apprenticeship test.

Cutting the engine, she reached over to the passenger seat to retrieve her copy of *Wild Edible and Medicinal Plants of the Pacific Northwest.* She was more familiar with gardens than wilderness, but her mom had sent her to summer camp every year of her childhood, and the forest didn't daunt her.

Tapping her phone, she opened her GPS app and pinned her current location so she could find her way back, then tucked it and the book into a reusable grocery bag alongside a small trowel, a pair of purple and yellow gardening gloves, and a compact rain poncho. She looked around as she stepped out of the car, taking in a circle of stones around an overgrown fire pit. The mossy log seats around it obviously hadn't been disturbed in quite a while, and knee-high saplings and brush filled the clearing.

Locking the car even though she doubted she needed to, she headed toward what looked like a trail on the uphill side of the clearing. According to her book, wild rhodiola rosea grew on rocky slopes at high altitudes.

She set off between the trees, scanning the surrounding plants for signs of fleshy rhodiola leaves. A thick layer of dry leaves and twigs crunched under her feet, birds sang overhead, and in the distance a woodpecker tatted out a rhythm. She let out a contented sigh, running her fingertips over the smooth gray trunk of a quaking aspen as she passed.

A scraggly thicket of salmonberries crowded the trail, and she sampled a few, letting the sweet juice coat her tongue. A mosquito buzzed her ear, and she reached into her bag for her homemade insect repellant. She wasn't yet much good at magical potions, but she had a decent grasp of essential oils, and her minty-citrus concoction not only worked, it smelled good. After dousing herself, she tucked the small spray bottle away and continued on.

The path grew steeper, making her calves burn as she climbed until she reached a sharp turn. To her right, the trail paralleled the top of a rocky ridge, but about fifteen feet below, she spotted a clump of rosette shaped leaves. *Rhodiola?* She stepped toward the edge to get a better look.

The ground beneath her feet collapsed. Too startled to even scream, she bumped and slithered helplessly down the incline on her backside, coming to a stop among a rain of pebbles and dust.

More stunned than hurt, she sat up and pushed her strawberry blonde hair out of her face before struggling to her feet. Other than a few scrapes and a racing heartbeat, she wasn't hurt, thank the Goddess. Next to her, scaly rosettes of rhodiola crouched staunchly among the rocks. Amidst the dust, her minty-citrus scented insect repellant had become cloying. She pulled the crushed bottle from her bag and wrinkled her nose. Oily residue covered everything inside. She wiped her phone and the book on the leg of her jeans. At least she'd be insect-free for a while.

Along the cliff face behind her, a scoured swath of dirt and stone showed her path down the steep incline. It was a wonder she wasn't seriously injured. She peered both directions along the wall. Not one spot looked possible to climb.

"Fuck," she muttered. Her stutter never affected her curse words.

She turned back to the rhodiola. *Might as well make the most of the situation before I try to climb back up.* She pulled out her book to make sure the photos matched, then put on her gardening gloves and shoved a clump aside to get at the root. The plant seemed to grow directly from a crack in one of the large stones. If she could've used store-bought herbs, she would've, but for this potion, the rhodiola root had to be freshly gathered within seventy-two hours after a full moon.

Jabbing the pointed end of her trowel into the crack, she tried to pry it apart, but the tool scraped uselessly against the stone. She tried several angles, but the ground refused to give up its hold on the plant. Standing upright, she glared toward the overcast sky in frustration.

As if the heavens were laughing at her, a fat raindrop hit her square on the forehead. *Great.*

She wiped at the moisture with the back of one wrist, moving on to another nearby plant. All she succeeded in doing was breaking a fingernail down to the quick and snapping a few stems off at ground level. "I need these damn roots."

How could this be so hard? Her trowel didn't give her enough leverage against the rocks. She would have to come back with a full-sized shovel and try again. At least she knew where the rhodiola was now.

Stuffing her trowel and gloves back into her bag, she pulled out her phone to mark the spot on her app.

No reception.

She held the phone overhead and paced a few feet in either direction, waiting for a signal. The app refused to come up. Maybe the rock wall was blocking her. *God, what a day.*

Well, as long as she didn't stray from the wall, she wouldn't end up walking in circles. Eventually, she'd get reception again. Or at least find a relatively easy spot to climb and get back to the trail.

Phone in hand, she began walking along the base of the cliff.

Adrian stopped his ATV next to a blue Subaru Forester and cut the engine. What was a car doing so far off the road? He dismounted and circled the vehicle. Judging by the tire tracks, it'd only been here a few hours. A single set of footprints—a woman's, he'd guess by the size—headed straight toward a game trail that led to the moose kill site. He'd need to hurry if he wanted to catch her before she reached it.

He shouldered his rifle and started off, yearning for the ease of his mountain lion form. Where the trail veered to follow a ridge, a swath of fresh dirt marred the edge. Cautious of an undercut, he edged closer and peered over the drop-off. That landslide was definitely not the product of a controlled descent, but he didn't see a body. He called out, "Hello, anyone down there?"

Only wind rustling the leaves responded.

Sniffing the breeze, he tried to detect if the woman was still nearby. A delicious odor wafted toward him, masking all other scents and making his inner feline wriggle. *Catnip?* How strange.

Since the footprints ended here, he would have to investigate. He clambered down using his hands and feet. Descending as a mountain lion would've been easier, but approaching a frightened hiker as a predator was never a good idea, let alone one as rare as a mountain lion.

At the bottom, the strong essence of catnip made his feline instincts claw for attention. Reigning in his desire to shed his clothing and roll around on his back, he found the scuff marks of the woman's shoes and followed her trail.

Loose sand and random boulders made walking difficult, but the trail of catnip led him forward even when the footprints weren't clear. At a large tree, several limbs had been freshly broken, as if the woman had tried to climb up.

The scent of catnip was stronger here, as well as the delicious scent of female. Floral with a hint of sweet black tea, it reminded him of his early days with his mother, before his mountain lion had emerged, before the pack rejected him. A mountain lion didn't belong among wolves. He was what they called a "sport," an offspring with unexpected traits inherited from a long-ago ancestor.

The female scent in the area made his uniform trousers feel uncomfortably tight. *Mate,* his mountain lion purred. Adrian's balls agreed, but his head knew better. The catnip had to be messing with his senses. While he appreciated human females, he'd never met one who made him want to claim her. He was thinking about claiming this one sight-unseen.

And the heady scent was powerful, driving him forward even more than his duty to protect a hiker.

Ahead, another tree had four deep gouges staining the papery white trunk with lines of sap. *Claws.* This was a fresh bear marking. Adrian sniffed the air, senses muddied by warm female and dizzying catnip. The grizzly shifter had been here. Had made this mark. But something was off about the scent, a cloying, ashy odor that made bile rise in Adrian's throat. Randall's warning about an infection returned.

Running his tongue over his lengthening canines, Adrian unslung his rifle and unlocked the safety. The female ahead was in danger. *My female,* his cat rumbled. Adrian couldn't deny the instinct. He picked up his pace to a run.

CHAPTER FOUR

$\mathcal{D}$arcy had changed her mind; she hated nature. From now on, she was sticking to cultivated herbs for her potions. No more of this wild herb bullshit.

How far had she walked? The sun poked feebly through the cloud cover, making it feel as if evening was approaching, although her phone said it was only two o'clock. The cliff was just as high as before, and she still didn't have a cell signal.

Her chest tightened. No one knew she was out here, not even Aunt Willow. No one would miss her until she didn't show up for her coven test in two days, and even then, they'd probably assume she chickened out.

"Fuuuck!" She batted at a spider web blocking her way and glanced once more at the steep cliff face. Thinking she might be able to shimmy along a branch to reach the cliff top, she'd tried to climb a tree a ways back, but the lower limbs had been too spindly to support her weight.

She whimpered as her ankle twisted for the millionth time on a loose rock. Ahead, the trees gave way. Maybe she could get a cell signal there. She limped forward, breaking into a clearing full of chest-high bushes interspersed with blackened prongs of what had once been trees.

Pulling out her cell again, she checked her signal. Not even half a bar. She groaned and turned once more to the cliff. How could there not be a single place she could climb? Maybe she should turn back and try the other direction.

Something grunted behind her. She spun, facing the sea of bushes.

A massive, dark shape with a wide head rose among the foliage about a hundred feet away. She took in its small ears, beady eyes, and huge paws. Her heart slammed against her ribcage.

A bear.

She wanted to scream, but her voice stuck in her throat. Was that a black bear or a grizzly? She'd grown up in Anchorage, and was technically an Alaska girl, but had never come face-to-face with the state's mightiest predator. All she knew was that for one kind of bear you fought back, and the other you played dead. Before she could decide which to do, the bear opened its mouth and roared.

"Oh, fuck!" She stumbled backward, feet slipping on the rocky slope. She fell to her ass against the stony ground, phone clattering from her hand.

The bear dropped to all fours and charged toward her with unbelievable speed, feet thumping against the earth like a drum.

Darcy screamed again, feet churning uselessly against the rocks. She grabbed a handful of pebbles and threw them as the bear broke from the shrubs a few feet away. Flinging her arms up to cover her face, she glimpsed a golden shape streaking in from the side.

It slammed into the bear, bowling it sideways and tumbling into the bushes. A wide swath of brush flattened in their wake. Darcy lowered her arms, gaping at the entangled creatures. The second beast was almost as large as the first, its long, golden tail lashing as it snarled and clawed the other predator. *Do we even have mountain lions in Alaska?*

The animals circled each other, fangs bared, ears laid back. Lunging forward, the bear struck with one giant paw. The big cat sprang straight up, out of the way. He landed on the bear's shoulders, sinking his fangs into its neck.

With a deafening bellow, the bear reared, shaking the lion off. The lion twisted and landed on its feet. Facing off, they circled again, snarling and lunging.

I have to get out of here. Darcy pushed upright, palms stinging and sticky with blood from where she'd fallen against the rocks. A jolt of blinding pain shot up her ankle, and it suddenly refused to take her weight. Breathing shallowly, she leaned one palm against the cliff and hop-stepped back the direction she'd come.

The mountain lion appeared to be driving the bear away, pursuing it toward the trees at the other end of the slope. Darcy had no idea how she'd been lucky enough to have two predators decide to duke it out with each other instead of have her for a snack, but she wasn't about to complain.

She tripped over a root, collapsing to her hands and knees. The sound of battle had ceased, and for a moment, she held still listening. Was it too much to hope they'd forgotten she was here? Maybe she should just crawl away so they wouldn't see her over the bushes. She lifted her head, aiming for the tree line.

Her gaze connected with the tawny golden eyes of the mountain lion. He crouched less than an arm's length away, muzzle stained crimson and one ear torn. She jolted backward, toppling onto her backside like a crab. *This is it. The end.* No one would even find her body because the lion would drag her off and eat her.

The lion prowled forward, a deep purr vibrating the air. His golden eyes mesmerized her, and her heart thundered so hard, she couldn't breathe. She found herself unable to look away.

He stepped forward slowly, gracefully, until his front paws straddled her. She was forced to lie back to avoid bumping noses. Barely breathing, she lay beneath him, the heat of his body radiating against her.

"N-nice kitty," she whispered.

He continued purring, lowering his face to rub his cheek against hers.

She cringed, expecting fangs. Only the rough prickle of his whiskers rubbed her skin. With trembling hands, she pushed his head away, the tawny fur lush and soft against her palms.

The big cat responded by purring louder. His golden eyes held an intelligence she hadn't expected. Why wasn't he tearing into her? Could he be somebody's pet? She dug her fingers into the thick fur and the tight fear in her chest eased a bit.

A long rough tongue snaked out to taste her throat, sending a surprisingly sensual shiver through her. She lay perfectly still as the lion moved down her body, snuffling and licking and rubbing. Was he marking her? She knew nothing about mountain lions.

He lifted a wide paw and placed it on her belly, kneading gently without baring his claws. Her skin quivered under the touch. He nudged his head up the inside of her thigh until he reached her center, hot breath penetrating her jeans.

She gasped, belly tightening around unexpected butterflies. *Oh, God.* She'd never had a fetish for animals, but this lion…

The cat lifted his head, intelligent gaze connecting to hers. He seemed to be considering. After several heartbeats, the air between them shimmered. The cat's features grew hazy, muzzle flattening and ears receding. The furry hide smoothed, and the limbs lengthened. Within moments, the beast was replaced by a tawny-haired, golden-eyed man kneeling between her legs. His hands were planted on the ground on either side of her thighs, every naked square inch of him rippling with muscle.

In a voice like a roll of thunder, he asked, "Why do you reek of catnip?"

CHAPTER FIVE

When Adrian had seen the grizzly, his mountain lion seized control before he could even aim his rifle, charging forward in catnip-driven recklessness. Now his clothing was shredded and he was drunk on catnip, inches from the most enchanting woman he'd ever encountered. Bits of leaves and sticks snarled her strawberry blonde hair, and her wide blue eyes met his. "What a-are you?"

Her stuttered words caused a surge of emotion inside him, a possessiveness he was not used to feeling. *Mine.* He wanted to lick every square inch of her. To rub his own scent across her curvaceous body. To fill her with his seed and make her his in every way possible. His mountain lion was growling *mate* over and over in his head. It had to be the catnip. The potent scent blocked even the rank stink of bear, confusing his senses, making his head swim as if he'd been roofied. He couldn't even detect what kind of shifter she was. Was she in heat? Why else would she have perfumed herself in catnip and come to his territory?

He crawled up her body, bringing his mouth within range of hers. Securing one of his knees between her legs, he pressed his thigh hard against the heat of her crotch. His cock pulsed with urgency, wanting her wet warmth wrapped around him. "Are you looking for me?"

She shook her head, both palms braced flat against his chest. Her jaw trembled. "I-I don't even know what you are."

He searched her blue eyes but found no guile. As he focused, the acrid smell of her fear carved a path through the other smells, sobering him. "Then why the catnip?"

"I-insect repellant. The b-bottle broke," she choked out, her attention shifting beyond his shoulder. "Is the bear gone?"

The bear. He lifted his head toward the crushed trail of alder bushes. A grizzly would normally have been more than a match for Adrian's mountain lion, but the scent of the terrified female had given Adrian a ferocity he'd never thought possible. The rogue now lay with his throat ripped out. At least any human stumbling upon the dead bear would assume it had died in a fight with another predator. He pressed the tip of his tongue against the fangs that kept trying to emerge and shook his head. He hoped Randall had been wrong about a rogue infection.

He'd figure that out later. Right now he had this female to deal with. "The bear's no longer a threat. What's your name?"

"D-Darcy."

"Darcy." He let her name roll off his tongue, drinking her in, fascinated by the way her lips moved. His mountain lion refused to disentangle himself from her. "I'm Adrian."

Her pretty throat moved with a swallow, and she slid one hand from his chest to touch the stubble on his chin, as if doubting he was real. "What kind of witch are you?"

Shivers raced through him. That was the smell he couldn't place. Ozone. She'd been near a witch recently. He said, "I'm a shifter, not a witch."

"Oh," she said on an exhale, her sweet breath fanning his cheek. The acrid scent of fear shifted and a high, fleeting whiff of arousal reached him.

He turned his head to nuzzle against the inside of her wrist. It was taking everything he had not to succumb to his desire to claim her here and now. *Damn catnip.* Lips still brushing her skin, he asked, "Why are you out here in the forest alone, kitten?"

"Harvesting r-rhodiola." Her voice had a rough breathiness he found irresistible.

He rubbed against her wrist and felt dampness against his thigh where it remained between her legs. God, he wanted to taste her. He slid his cheek to the crook of her arm, tongue flicking against her tender, sensitive skin.

She gasped, and the scent of her arousal grew, but so did the acrid scent of fear. "Are you going to eat me?"

He wanted to tell her yes, in the best way possible. Woozy from catnip, he pulled himself under control and lifted his mouth from her skin, forcing himself to stand. "I would never harm you."

Her eyes grew rounder as her gaze flickered toward his erection. "W-why are you n-naked?"

Her adorable stutter was more pronounced as she obviously tried not to look at his crotch—and failed miserably. Part of him liked the attention, but it was making it difficult to stay off of her. He kept picturing her plump, red mouth around his shaft. He glanced around for something to cover himself while he growled out, "Kind of difficult to wear clothes as a mountain lion."

She returned her attention to his face, a pink flush rising to her cheeks. "W-would you like to borrow my rain poncho?" She pulled a bag from her shoulder and produced a cheap green emergency poncho.

"Thank you." He accepted the packet and shook out the thin plastic before wrapping it around his hips like a kilt. A huge tent rose over his crotch. He gestured downward. "I can't do anything about that. It has a mind of its own."

A giggle escaped her, breaking the tension between them. Her smile was like a sunrise, and a giddy sensation welled up inside him. It reminded him of the stories his father used to tell about meeting his mother. How the pack had never felt like home until he'd bonded with her.

He clamped down on the memory. Packs were for werewolves. Mountain lions lived alone.

"Come." He offered her a hand. "I'll show you back to your car."

"You know a way back up the cliff?" She put her delicate palm into his, and he pulled her onto her feet.

"Of course. This is my territory."

She took one limping step and stumbled against him, her full breasts soft against his arm. A purr rose in his chest. She was round and soft in all the right places, yet solid enough to be a worthy mate. *Mine.* The word flitted through him again.

"I t-twisted my ankle," she said.

Without waiting for permission, he swept her into his arms. "I'll carry you."

She gasped, clutching his neck. "I'm too heavy!"

"You aren't heavy." In fact, she felt like a feather in his arms, fitting perfectly against his chest. He strode along the cliff to where a stream cut a trail, heart beating faster than carrying her warranted.

CHAPTER SIX

*D*arcy clung to Adrian as he stalked toward the trees. He smelled of pine, wood smoke and hot-blooded male, and the heat of his naked chest against her made her insides clench with need. Now was not the time or place to feel horny, but damn if this guy wasn't some sort of sex-god. *No, he's a shifter.* She'd never met one, but the other witches talked about shifters as if they were barely controlled animals who argued until they drew blood. How could she have mistaken him for a witch? *Not only does my stutter ruin every spell, I can't even tell shifters from witches.* She felt like the stupidest witch on the planet.

They reached a tiny stream trickling down the cliff, and her stomach lurched as he leapt upward from ledge to ledge without breaking his stride. *Damn, he's nimble.* His gait barely even jostled her aching ankle.

She forced herself to loosen her chokehold on him. Mountain lion, mountain man, this guy was hot.

His nostrils flared, and she wondered if he could smell her pheromones. Which only turned her on more. *What the hell is wrong with me?* You'd think she was a cat in heat.

His chest vibrated with a growl. "Don't do that."

She looked into his face. "What?"

"I can smell your arousal. It's as distracting as catnip."

Oh, shit, he *could* smell her. And that only made her core clench tighter. She looked away, focusing on the trail ahead to avoid his gaze. She didn't want to stutter out some lame excuse and embarrass herself any more than she already had. *Stupid sexy shifter.*

They reached the top of the ridge and he threaded his way through the trees with unerring confidence. "Why are you looking for rhodiola?"

She swallowed, gathering her words on her tongue before speaking. "I'm making a potion."

"You're making it?" He bent his face closer and inhaled deeply, which was weird but also kind of sexy.

"Yes," she said with more confidence than she felt.

A frown creased his brow. "You don't smell like a witch. Not exactly."

His words created a hollow in her chest, an echo of all the times her mother told her she had no natural talent for witchcraft. If it wasn't for Aunt Willow, Darcy wouldn't even know a coven existed. Not that she had a hope in hell of getting them to teach her anything, not at the rate she was going. She had no idea how she would get her hands on some fresh rhodiola root between now and her test day after tomorrow. Her throat hurt with the effort of controlling words tangled by emotions. "What d-do I smell like, then?"

His lip twitched, revealing a sharp canine that made her heart race. "I'm uncertain."

"Well, I'm n-not a shapeshifter, that's for sure."

He raised one eyebrow. "Would that be so bad?"

She bit her lip, realizing she'd just insulted him. "N-no."

His nostrils flared, but he didn't remark, swiveling to avoid catching her feet against a long evergreen bough.

The trees soon opened into the clearing where her car was parked. Next to it sat an ATV with a Forestry Service logo on the side. Adrian set her on the ATV's padded black seat.

"This is y-yours?" She'd imagined him as a wild mountain man, not a Forestry official.

"I'm a ranger." He dropped to his knees in front of her

and slid his calloused hands behind her calf, drawing her leg toward him. "How's your ankle?"

Rockets of anticipation shot up her leg to her insides. How could he continually have such a carnal effect on her? She cleared her throat, preparing to tell him it was fine, but then he rotated her ankle, and she yelped.

"Sorry. It doesn't look broken, but it's definitely sprained." He'd been gentle, but damn, that hurt. He stood and rummaged through a box on the back of his ATV. "I have a bandage in here somewhere."

Even though her ankle throbbed, she was mesmerized by his lithe grace. His arms were well-proportioned muscle, bulging and flexing as he moved, and the broad cobra shape of his back made her want to run her palms along his ribs to his narrow hips and gorgeous ass.

He returned with a first aid kit, and with surprising dexterity and gentleness removed her shoe and sock. Every time his fingertips brushed her skin, it was as if her whole being cried out for more. As he wrapped her ankle, she could almost think he'd cast a spell on her. Except shifters didn't cast spells.

He finished and rose. The poncho tented over the front of his hips remained as pronounced as ever, and part of her wished she hadn't asked him to cover himself.

"Thank you for your help," she said, pleased when she didn't stutter.

His golden eyes seemed to glow in the dim forest light. "You're welcome. Can you drive?"

"I th-think so." She pushed herself onto her good foot, but before she could take another step, he'd scooped her up again.

"Keys?"

She dug awkwardly in her bag and retrieved them. He carried her to the driver's side door and gently lowered her feet to the ground, maintaining one arm around her waist for support. She unlocked the car and opened the door, but instead of sitting, she turned and wrapped her arms around his neck. He'd saved her, but for all she knew, she'd never see him again and she wanted to do this before she lost her nerve. Raising herself on the toes of her good foot, she kissed him solidly on the mouth.

Much to her surprise, he slid one hand up her back to cup her neck, keeping their lips together. The firm tip of his erection nudged her belly, drawing the butterflies in her stomach downward. He tasted so good, lips softer than she would've imagined. He moved them slowly against hers, sliding his tongue into her just once before pulling away.

Confidence boosted, she let out a slow breath and opened her eyes. "W-would you like to come to dinner at my house? It's the least I can do."

Wow, that had been a long sentence. More words than she usually strung together at once. And she'd barely stuttered at all.

To her relief, he smiled, showing a tiny bit more teeth than most people showed, but his hands were a warm comfort on her hips. "I'd be delighted."

He said yes! Flustered and excited, she plopped down in the driver's seat and jabbed the key into the ignition. Her trusty Subaru started right up. There were so many things she needed to do to get ready. Her house was a mess, for one thing, and she needed to wash her sheets. Plus, she was out of mascara. She hoped the Trading Post had some.

He rested one forearm on the top of the open door, showing no inclination to step back and close it. Had she forgotten something? She met his gaze, and his eyes sparked with a feral desire that made her insides tighten.

"I can probably track you down by the trail of catnip, but it would be much easier if you gave me your address, kitten."

Heat filled her face. She'd never had a pet name before, and he kept calling her kitten in a way that made her want to roll over and show him her belly. Or her naked pussy. Geez, the guy gave her a one-track mind. She stammered out directions, and he nodded, closing the car door and stepping out of the way.

She bumped her way down the rutted road, watching the rearview mirror until he was hidden by brush. Then it hit her. What the hell did you feed a mountain lion for dinner?

CHAPTER SEVEN

*A*drian watched the Subaru disappear and stood listening to the fading engine until he was certain Darcy'd reached the road. With the allure of catnip gone, he took a moment to reassess the emotions roiling through him. Her kiss had surprised him, started a fire inside him that could only be quenched by her—preferably her warm wet pussy around his cock. He'd scratched his carnal itch a time or two with human females, but never imagined himself with a mate. *She's my mate.* His mountain lion was certain of it.

But she claimed she was a witch. Could a shifter even claim a witch? Interbreeding sometimes happened—his mountain lion was proof of that, and in high school he could recall several scandalous rumors of a young pack-mate getting caught making out with a vampire.

But supernaturals generally kept to their own kind, and claiming a mate was far more serious than a high school crush. For the first time in a long time, he missed belonging to a pack, missed the glint in his oldest brother's eyes when he'd shared naughty rumors with the younger siblings.

But that had been before Adrian knew he was different. Before his feline had revealed itself and forced Adrian into solitude, unable to accept a pack-Alpha's bond. *Now you want a mate?*

The mountain lion inside of him rumbled assent.

Adrian could only shake his head. He loved a lot of things about his mountain lion, but its unpredictable nature was not one of them. Once he got Darcy out of his bloodstream, they'd see what his lion thought.

Removing the clingy plastic poncho from around his waist, he tucked it into the box on his ATV and pulled out his spare uniform. He needed to retrieve his phone and rifle, then file his report. The sooner he got that out of the way, the sooner he could get to Darcy's.

He followed the trail back to the cliff and descended to where he'd shed his clothes. There was little left of his uniform, but he gathered his keys, phone, and rifle before investigating the corpse. The grizzly lay as he'd left it, sprawled in the dense shrubbery, brown furry throat matted with blood. The musky stink of the shifter was even worse after death, but there was also a note of something else, that ashy scent he'd noted before. *Illness?*

Adrian felt a twinge of regret over the shifter; rogues usually had a sad story leading up to their descent into madness, often events beyond their control. He took several photos, making note of the distinguishing white patches of fur, one on the base of the bear's skull and another just behind its left shoulder-blade. Both were over what a hunter would consider kill spots, as if the bear had been marked for death. *Odd.* Hopefully, the marks would help the shifter's den-mates identify the body quickly and provide closure for loved ones.

Out of respect, he placed a few broken shrubs over the body to conceal it from prying eyes and headed back toward the ridge. As he reached the base, he noticed a squat stand of wild rhodiola not too far away. Wasn't that what Darcy'd been gathering? He didn't recall seeing or smelling any herbs on her except the catnip. She might appreciate a few roots if she hadn't managed to gather any.

Glancing around to be sure no one was nearby, he shimmied out of his clothing and shifted, using his claws to make short work of the rocky soil around the plant. After unearthing several roots, he shifted back and dressed before climbing up to his waiting ATV.

Back at his cabin, he called Randall. "We don't need to file an extermination report with the Forest Service," he added. "There were no bullets involved. You can tell the Den to come claim their dead."

A beat of silence. "What the hell, Adrian? You took on a grizzly while shifted?"

"I got the drop on him while he was attempting another kill." For some reason, Adrian didn't want to mention Darcy. His emotions around her were too raw, and for now, he wanted to keep her to himself. It was enough that he'd done his duty with the rogue. "There was definitely something wrong with him, though. He smelled and tasted like ash."

"You were supposed to use your rifle. We don't know what's causing this outbreak. Now you could be infected."

Adrian gritted his teeth. "I feel fine." He thought about the ashy taste the bear had left in his mouth. "I'll let you know if I get any symptoms."

"Very funny, Adrian. A rogue isn't going to report himself going rogue. Seriously, there will be a lot of questions. The Council will want an inquisition."

An inquisition meant he'd have to show up at the local bar where the shifters held their meetings. "You know I hate going into town."

"It'll give you a chance to catch up on your emails," Randall said, sarcasm dripping from his words. "Keep your phone handy so I can reach you."

"Fine." All Adrian wanted to do was hang up so he could get ready for dinner with Darcy. He'd deal with rogue infection threats later. "Oh, and the grizzly had some white markings that might make it easier to identify him. I'm forwarding you some photos from my phone."

"All right." Randall sighed. "Good job, by the way."

Adrian grunted and hung up, then went to the stream behind his cabin to scrub up.

CHAPTER EIGHT

Darcy stopped by the Trading Post to pick up something for dinner. The small store didn't have a lot of selection, but Karl, the owner, carried meat in the freezer. Men and mountain lions were both bound to like a steak, right?

A metal shelf bisected the small grocery, and the pegboard wall behind the register held an assortment of hardware and auto parts. A glass case full of Native artwork supported a cash register where Karl's gray head was bent over a book.

"Hi, Karl," she said as she entered, hobbling on her injured ankle.

He set his book down. "What happened to you, sweetie?"

"A sp-sprain." She stopped at the counter, glancing toward the freezer cases in the back. "D-do you have steak?"

Karl rose and headed toward the storeroom door. "Let me check. I stopped keeping the expensive stuff up front 'cause it kept getting stolen." He disappeared into the back room.

Darcy examined the pegboard, checking the price on the long-handled shovel hanging there, but found it hard to focus. *He rescued me from a bear!* The witches in the coven would never consider befriending a shifter, let alone asking one on a date, but Darcy couldn't stop thinking about Adrian's golden-eyed gaze and the way his mouth had felt when she'd kissed him. And he was obviously attracted to her. The erection he'd sported the entire time they'd been together couldn't be denied —he'd even joked about it, which she found remarkably endearing.

She remembered she needed mascara and limped over to the shelf bins where Karl stocked a few bargain-basement cosmetics. The bell over the door jangled, and she looked up at a woman in a billowy blouse with a long auburn braid. *Aunt Willow.* Her smile died. Darcy'd been seventeen when Mom died, and Aunt Willow had stepped in as a surrogate, teaching her about witchcraft and attempting to correct her stutter. But neither magic nor physical therapy had helped. Darcy definitely didn't want to get caught up in conversation with her aunt right now, but it was too late.

"Darcy? What happened to you?" Aunt Willow's gaze darted to Darcy's bandaged foot. "Are you injured?"

"J-just s-sprained." Only two words, but she stuttered them both. Talking to Aunt Willow always seemed to make the problem worse.

Her aunt advanced, pursing her lips in disapproval. "Well, it's nothing a little spell won't fix."

With a quick glance toward the back where Karl could be heard moving around, Aunt Willow leaned over and brushed her fingertips over the bandage, speaking some barely audible words. The pain in Darcy's ankle turned to ice, then disappeared as if it had never been there.

Standing upright once more, her aunt crossed her arms over her ample bosom. "There. Quite simple."

Darcy's throat tightened at the subtext—that she must lack the willpower to succeed. "Th-thank you."

"You look like you've been rolling around at the zoo." Aunt Willow's red manicured fingernails snatched a bit of moss from Darcy's hair. "And you smell like you fell in a vat of horse liniment. No wonder the coven is on the fence about you."

Nausea filled Darcy's belly. She hadn't even taken the test yet. "Th-they are?"

"Don't worry. I assured them you won't follow in your mother's footsteps."

Mom had been a coven member during her early years, but had divorced herself from her fellow witches and moved to Anchorage before Darcy was born. Darcy hadn't even met her aunt until the funeral, and no one would tell her why mom left.

Willow leaned closer, glancing over her shoulder to be certain Karl wasn't in earshot. "But when you show up in public like this, you make me look like a liar."

Heat filled Darcy's face. Her aunt was determined to restore the family's reputation by getting Darcy into the coven, and Darcy was terrified about letting her down.

Karl reappeared carrying a frozen vac-pack of meat. "Hey, there, Willow."

Darcy thrust two twenties at him and took the package, ignoring his call that she'd forgotten her change as she rushed from the store. What was she thinking? She shouldn't be taking time for a date when she should be working on her potion. But she'd failed to gather the rhodiola, and although there was still plenty of Alaskan summer daylight, the rain had begun in earnest, pounding hard against her windshield as she drove toward home. *I'll head out first thing tomorrow.* And this time she'd take a real shovel. Maybe she could convince Adrian to help her.

She pulled to a stop on the gravel driveway of the house she was renting, dodging puddles as she sprinted for the front door. Her wet clothes still smelled like insect repellant, and she tossed them in the washer before heading to the shower and lathering herself twice. At least her strawberry blonde hair no longer looked like a frayed broomstick, but her encounter with her aunt had her on edge. She couldn't shake the negative energy.

Performing a quick sage smudge around the living room made her feel slightly better, so she seasoned the steaks and scrubbed a couple of potatoes. She was growing a few heads of lettuce among her herb pots on the porch, and stepped into her Crocs to go outside and pick a salad, glad the rain had slowed to a misty drizzle. Someday, she wanted to have a house with a garden and a shed to dry her herbs, but for now, her pots worked. Running a frond of rosemary beneath her nose, she decided to use some for the steaks.

The rumble of an engine drew her attention as a dark green Ford pickup rolled into view. *Adrian?* He parked in the street and stepped out of the truck, looking handsome and well-groomed, broad shoulders straining ever so slightly against the white button-down shirt. He'd been gorgeous when naked, but Goddess, he rocked the clothing look, too.

Holding something in one hand, he prowled toward the porch. "Hello, kitten."

She loved the pet name, and the way his eyes reflected the light, making him seem dangerous and sexy. "C-come inside."

She led the way, stepping out of her shoes in the entryway.

He closed the door and thrust a plastic grocery bag toward her.

She accepted it and peered inside. Two perfectly gnarled roots lay twined together. She let out an awed breath. "Rhodiola?"

"My mountain lion wanted to bring you a dead rabbit." He untied his scuffed work boots. "I thought you might appreciate this more."

She hugged the roots to her chest. *Goddess, this guy is too good to be true.* Now she could focus on making the potion instead of spending tomorrow wandering around the forest. "You just saved my ass again. Thank you."

He set his boots next to her Crocs and faced her. "Next time you want to go walking in the woods, call me. I'll give you an escort."

The fluttering in her stomach intensified. "I b-bet you say that to all the girls."

His eyes glowed in the light coming through her living room windows. "I don't talk to other girls."

Feeling light and warm, she carried the roots to her kitchen. "Do you want wine?"

A tiny smile flitted across his mouth and he tilted his head. "No catnip?"

Her insides fluttered with uncertainty. "D-do you want catnip?"

He grinned and shook his head. "I'm only teasing. Wine would be great."

God, he was stunning when he smiled. She could barely catch her breath as her stomach flip-flopped. Glad to have something else to focus on, she poured two glasses and handed him one.

He took a sip. "Your home is nice."

"Thanks." She dampened some paper towels and wrapped the rhodiola before placing it into her crisper drawer. Tomorrow, she'd make the potion. But tonight, she was going to thank this hunky ranger for his help, even if it meant making small talk. "D-do you live here in town?"

"No, I live in a ranger cabin out in the park."

"Are there other m-mountain lions living in the park?"

A sardonic smile curled his lip. "I'm the only one I know of."

"Oh." She frowned. "I thought shifters had packs."

Adrian's smile transformed into a fanged grimace. "Packs are for wolves."

Startled at the scary transformation, she sucked in a breath. "S-sorry."

His face softened, and he sighed. "My parents are from the pack in Gakona."

She gaped. "W-wolves? But you're... How'd that happen?"

"If a bloodline is impure—if it has another shifter type in its ancestry—a different shifter type can be produced. The mountain lion form is recessive. The pack didn't want me."

"They rejected you?" she asked softly, knowing exactly how he felt.

He licked his lips and looked into his glass. "It's for the best. Mountain lions prefer solitude."

Darcy took a deep gulp of wine. "But you're here. With me."

He lifted his chin. "You're... different."

Usually to her, different meant bad, but he made it seem like a good thing. "I'm n-not really a witch. That's why I need the potion."

He canted his head. "How's a potion going to help? I thought you either were a witch or you weren't."

Closing her eyes and picturing the words before she spoke, she said, "My m-mom was a witch, and so's my aunt. My stutter ruins my spells. The p-potion will cure it." Goddess, she hoped that was true. "At least long enough to p-pass the coven's tests."

"But isn't the potion itself magic? If you can make it, that seems like it should be proof enough."

She shook her head. "They have specific tests for apprentices. Not just any human with a spark of magic can join."

"And what will joining the coven give you?"

"M-mentors."

"You mean teachers?" He raised his eyebrows. "Can't your aunt or your mom just teach you?"

"M-my mother is dead. And my aunt tried. But m-my stutter..." she trailed off, waving one hand as if that explained everything.

"I'm sorry." His gaze on her remained steady, not like he expected her to speak, but as if he understood. He wasn't finishing her sentence for her, just listening and letting her set the pace. She wasn't certain if that gave her more confidence or less.

Uncomfortable with the turn of conversation, she retrieved the steaks from the fridge. "Do you like b-bar-b-be—" She took a steadying breath. "Barbecue?"

He nodded once. "Rare, please."

Of course he wants rare. Smiling, she carried the steaks toward the balcony.

CHAPTER NINE

$\mathcal{A}$drian followed Darcy outside onto the small porch, admiring the sway of her ass in her jeans and the way her green tee shirt hugged her curves. She said she wasn't a witch yet, but she'd certainly bewitched him. The coven's tests weren't fair if they would penalize her for stuttering.

The porch was barely ten feet across and filled with pots of various herbs. A small folding table held a tabletop propane grill. From here, he could see the edge of her neighbor's house across the street, but trees mostly blocked the other widely-spaced homes. Even so, the sounds and smells of nearby people were almost overwhelming. Next door, a baseball game played on the television, and somewhere nearby a rhubarb pie had just come out of the oven. Part of Adrian missed having a community, but his mountain lion would never put up with having people this close all the time.

Darcy's deliciously floral scent mixed with the herbs on her porch helped ground him amidst the whirlwind of sensory input. He set his wineglass on the porch rail and moved in close behind her while she adjusted the flame to preheat the grill.

She shut the lid and turned, colliding with his chest. "Oh!" Her luscious mouth fluttered into a hesitant smile. "Excuse me."

"You're beautiful when you smile." He used one finger to brush a wisp of hair out of her eyes.

Arousal spiked the air and a delectable flush infused her pale freckled skin. Bending, he feathered his lips over hers. She responded warmly, accepting his tongue when it dipped into her sweetness. He delved one hand into the soft hair at her nape, pulling her deeper into the kiss, while his other hand rested gently on her hip.

As he languidly explored her mouth, her nipples grew hard against his chest. Damn, he wanted her naked so he could sample all of her.

Children's voices cut the air as two youngsters biked past on the dirt road. Darcy pulled away, glancing that direction before turning once more to the grill. "This should b-be hot now."

Was he moving too fast? He didn't know and didn't care. He'd been with a few women, humans, to satisfy his needs when the opportunity arose, but he'd never been as driven to have one as he was now. His cock was more demanding than his stomach at the moment. He pressed himself against Darcy's backside before she could place the meat on the grill.

She sucked in a breath, hand hovering above on the grill's lid. Her back arched as her ass contacted his erection. She leaned back until her shoulder blades met his chest. He could feel her rapid shallow breaths as she awaited his next move.

He was happy to oblige. Sliding both palms flat over her ribcage until his fingers met atop her belly, he secured her against him. She let her head fall back against his shoulder, allowing him access to her neck. Did she realize how damn sexy that was, yielding to his beast in the most primal of ways? His canines ached to come out, to place his claiming bite upon her shoulder. He dipped lower and put his lips against the skin just above her shirt collar, letting the tip of his tongue flicker against her skin.

Her entire body trembled. She slid both hands behind her, locating the line of his throbbing shaft through his slacks. Aching for more, he groaned, pumping his hips forward to catch her hands between them for a moment. She stroked his length, drawing him to excruciating hardness. He cupped her heavy breasts, thumbs finding her nipples and massaging them through her bra.

Nuzzling the nape of her neck, he imagined what it would feel like to take her from behind. She was making tiny noises of pleasure, and when her fingers fumbled at his belt buckle, he almost bit down then and there. *No, not like an animal.* He wouldn't claim her, only enjoy a night of pleasure if she would grant it. Anything more permanent was not possible, not for a loner like him.

He turned off the propane and pressed his mouth close to her ear. "I want you."

She nodded.

That was the only consent he needed. Spinning her to face him, he cupped her face in both hands and kissed her properly. Deeply. Possessively. Their tongues fought back and forth until she panted against him, her deft fingers opening buckle and zipper until his cock sprang free. She encircled him with a firm grip.

Aware of how exposed they were on the porch, he grasped her wrist, ceasing her movement. "Where's your bedroom, kitten?"

She blinked as if disoriented, then smiled. Taking his hand, she led him inside. "I th-thought you'd never ask."

CHAPTER TEN

*H*eart pounding, Darcy led Adrian through her living area to her queen-sized bed. She'd only been with a few guys, but none of them had ever made her feel the way Adrian could in only a few minutes. Her panties were damp—which she was certain he already knew—but she lay back on the bed, propped onto her elbows, and slowly opened her legs.

His tongue slid along his lips, giving her a glimpse of long canines. Those teeth should frighten her, but for some reason they only turned her on more. His features seemed unable to decide if he was a cat or a man, his face marked by lines of fur. She found him fascinating. Gorgeous.

Above his open fly, a fine line of dusky hair pointed from his navel to an erection the size of which she'd never seen. Wanting to taste him, she reached out and wrapped one hand around his shaft, drawing him close.

He grunted, hips flexing. Her fingers didn't quite meet as she encircled his girth, but she slid her grip up to the pulsing tip, letting her thumb run over a bead of pre-cum glistening at the slit. He growled with desire. Or was it a snarl?

She took the head of his cock in her mouth, rolling her tongue around the smooth velvet knob as she reached around to push his pants down his hips. He tasted masculine and sweet, and she opened wide to draw him in. Unable to take all of him, she encircled the base of his shaft with her hand and squeezed.

He groaned, threading both hands into the back of her hair and trembling with restraint as he obviously resisted the urge to thrust deeper. She worked his length, sucking and licking, curling her fingers around his heavy balls until he groaned and pushed her back against the bed. He slid the hem of her tee shirt upward, grazing her skin with his heated palm. His eyes seemed to glow with an almost feral light, and he lowered his face to her bared abdomen.

Taking a long inhale, he blew it out, raising goose bumps where his breath fanned her skin. His stubbled cheek met her bare abdomen with an electrifying jolt. Heat raced from her bellybutton and settled on her clit.

She gasped, back arching. *Holy fuck, he's good.*

His big palms unhooked her bra and cupped her breasts as he grazed his chin against her. She could feel him humming. *Purring.* He swiped his tongue in a broad path up to her ribcage.

She slid her hands to his mop of thick, tawny hair and groaned. His tongue continued lapping against her skin, driving her mad. Making her squirm.

He moved downward, supporting her lower back and drawing her against him, licking, sucking, nipping. The heat between her legs ached to feel that mouth. He neared the waistband of her jeans and growled, "Let's take these off."

She mutely nodded. *Oh, yes.* He could do anything he liked as long as he didn't stop with that tongue. Releasing her grip on his hair, she flicked open the button and lowered the zipper even as he tugged at the waistband. Before she knew it, she was down to her panties.

His pants had been discarded at some point she didn't remember, and he planted a bare knee firmly between her spread legs, placing both broad palms atop her thighs. His skin felt searingly hot against her, and she trembled, pussy tightening and legs widening.

She swallowed, enraptured by the pure magnificence of him, and tugged at his shirt. "I want to see you."

With dexterous fingers, he flicked open the buttons and shrugged free, exposing golden skin rippling over broadly muscled shoulders and abs. Heat flooded her panties.

His thumbs traced lazy circles against her inner thighs, making it hard to think straight. His pine forest musk reached her, and she wanted him like she'd never wanted another man. She looked into his tawny gaze, drowning in desire.

He smiled, attention trailing down her body to her panty-clad crotch. "I'm going to eat you."

Her chest tightened in alarm yet her hips automatically flexed upward, as if he'd just stroked her cleft.

In a swift move, he slid both thumbs beneath the thin crotch of her panties and with a snap, tore the fabric loose. Then he plunged his face between her legs. It was as if his entire mouth engulfed her pussy, long tongue circling her lower lips and sending a wave of dizzying desire through her. She made a strangled noise and tilted her head back, both hands tangling in his hair as he licked and stroked her until she was on the edge of climax.

She rocked her hips against him, catching a rhythm with his tongue against her clit. The quivering in her belly was growing almost painful, a rippling wave hovering just below the surface. Then his tongue penetrated her, going deep into her channel and stroking a spot that turned the sensation into a roaring wave.

With a cry, she convulsed around him. He didn't relent, pumping his tongue in and out of her until he'd lapped up every drop of her orgasm. She melted against the comforter, barely able to breathe.

He gave her pussy a final satisfied lick and then prowled up her body to hover above her, face-to-face. She could feel his breath on her, smell herself on him. Normally she'd shy away from her own odor, but mixed with his musk, it fanned her desire again. His huge cock rested against her inner thigh, a rod of heat she wasn't sure she could handle, yet wanted more than breath itself.

She looked into his eyes and gasped, "Take me."

He growled, flexing his hips until the swollen head pressed against her entrance. With maddening slowness, he filled her, stretching her tired muscles around him, easing forward in small in-and-out strokes that had her panting by the time he was fully seated inside her. She wrapped both arms around his lean waist. His skin felt like velvet, and she crept both hands over the solid mounds of his ass, pulling him closer, deeper.

He withdrew for a beat, chest heaving as he stared at her face. Then he slammed back into her. She cried out, riding the waves of her pleasure as he pounded out a rhythm as primal as the earth, stroking in and out, filling her, consuming her. Another climax built within her, promising more pleasure than the first.

This was perfect. Absolutely, mind bogglingly perfect. She felt the prick of his teeth against the top of her shoulder and she wanted the pain, craved it in a way she couldn't explain. She tilted her head, giving him more room.

"Harder," she begged.

He snarled, abs flexing powerfully as he rocked his hips, cock throbbing as if growing even bigger inside of her.

"Ohhh!" she moaned, her orgasm cresting. "Yes, do it!"

His teeth at her neck clamped down, and what should've been shockingly painful only intensified her pleasure. As his cock pulsed and his pace slowed, warmth pooled onto the bedding beneath her ass.

She gulped air, body trembling and satiated. Her hair was sticky against her neck and the smell of blood filled the air. She reached up, fingertips tracing the tender bite mark. Surprisingly, she didn't mind.

He caught her hand and lifted it, brows pinched. "You okay with this?"

She met his eyes, thinking he was the most perfect being she'd ever met. "I-I liked it."

"But will you tomorrow?" His frown remained firmly in place, sparking a thread of alarm in her.

"What do you mean? I'll heal."

"I claimed you." His eyes glowed with light that could only be magic.

The pit of her stomach flip-flopped. *Claimed? As in, bound us as mates?* "But I'm a witch."

Adrian rose, running a hand over his hair and pacing. "Fuck."

She sat up and pulled the edge of the comforter over her torso, heart slamming against her ribs as her sex-muddled thoughts cleared. She'd been bitten by a shifter. What did that mean for her magic? She'd never heard of a shifter witch before. As far as she knew, you could only be one or the other. "But I want to be a witch."

He paused his pacing and stared at her, then bent and snatched up his pants. "I have to go."

"W-wait!" She scrambled forward, following him into the living room with the comforter wrapped around her. How could he dress himself and walk at the same time? She could barely keep the comforter from tripping her, and he was already shoving his feet into his boots. "Why are you leaving?"

He spun to face her, his features tight and hands clenched at his sides. "You're perfect and amazing, but you don't want me and I can't take a mate. I will fix this, I promise."

With that, he flung open her apartment door and dashed to his truck.

Darcy pressed her hand over the wound on her shoulder, stomach churning as she listened to his tires kick up gravel. He'd left her. He'd marked her and left her. *Goddess, I'm so stupid.* Just because he'd saved her life and brought her gifts, didn't mean she could trust him with her body. Or her heart.

She closed the apartment door and retreated to the bathroom. In the mirror, the blood looked garish trickling down her pale freckled skin, but there was less of it than she'd feared. Grabbing a washcloth, she cleaned the wound. It had stopped bleeding, but would probably leave a scar. *A mark.* How was she going to explain this to her aunt?

Shifters and witches didn't mix. Period. Would the coven still accept her if they knew?

She closed her eyes and searched herself for a hint of shifter power. What would that feel like? She knew she had to go to the glacier and drink from a magical Source to acquire a shifter form, but would she sense it if an animal spirit was waiting for her? She tried to picture a gorgeous golden female mountain lion, but felt no different from before. *Even shifter magic avoids a girl with a stutter.*

Gritting her teeth, she glared into the mirror and repeated the words of one of her most recent speech therapists. "No. N-negative. Self-talk."

Adrian said he was going to fix this. Maybe there was a way to erase the bite. If not, she just had to hide the mark. which shouldn't be difficult. This was Alaska; between the bugs and the cold, it wasn't like she was prancing around in strapless sundresses, anyway. The coven never needed to know.

Besides, wasn't a claiming supposed to bond mates together? The way Adrian had rushed out of here, he obviously didn't have any warm fuzzies for her.

Regardless of how empty she felt with his absence.

CHAPTER ELEVEN

*A*drian didn't have a Pack or a Den or a Pride to turn to for advice like other shifters. Other than Randall, who he preferred to keep at arm's length, the only shifters he knew personally were his parents in Gakona. They were the last people he wanted to turn to, but he'd do it if there was a way to reverse this.

Tires throwing up mud, Adrian rounded the corner onto a dirt road spotted at regular intervals by long driveways. Between the thick trees, he could glimpse secluded houses, yards full of abandoned vehicle parts, a chicken coop...

God, I fucked up. He hadn't meant to bite Darcy, but when she demanded "harder," his feline instincts took over. His mountain lion wanted her, wanted to make her his, regardless of what Adrian's head was saying. He'd driven into her like a rutting beast, and his fangs had come out without a second thought. Now all he could think about was touching her again, tasting her again, holding her close the rest of the night. But that instinct wouldn't last. He knew himself better than that, and he'd want his space again, eventually. He wasn't a social creature.

Plus, she was a witch—or wanted to be.

"Shit shit shit." He pounded the steering wheel. He'd fucked up her life. If the claim could be reversed, he needed to figure it out now, before it became permanent.

He parked across the street from his parents' driveway and stared down the narrow lane to the pale yellow ranch-style house. It looked exactly as it always did during his random drive-bys over the years, with his mother's orange and yellow nasturtiums overflowing the half-barrel planters at the base of the concrete pad porch and filmy lace curtains drawn across the big living room windows. What if they turned him away?

He hadn't spoken to his family since they'd discovered he was a mountain lion and sent him to Anchorage to foster with a lion Pride when he was fifteen. A "boot camp for wayward shifter teens" they'd called it. Fuck that. He wasn't a savannah lion, he was a mountain lion, and his parents hadn't even known the difference. Pride or Pack, he didn't belong. After a few weeks of getting bullied by the Pride's Alpha, he'd run away.

The next few years Adrian lived on the street, avoiding Child Protective Services and attending class at King Career Center. His teacher had been a shifter, a black bear, who seemed to understand Adrian's need to be alone and do things for himself, and had helped Adrian get his diploma and secure this job with the Forestry Service after he turned eighteen.

Now, Adrian took a calming breath, got out of his car, and walked stiffly toward his parents' front door, stepping over the crack in the concrete he and his brothers used to pretend would curse you if you touched it. The inner door was open, and the scent of Mom's moose-burger casserole floated through the screen.

His hand hesitated over the door latch. *This isn't home anymore.* He couldn't just walk in unannounced. He didn't belong.

A familiar silhouette moved into view behind the screen and his father's voice scratched out, "Adrian?"

Dad wore his State Trooper uniform, his hair grayer but still the same neat trim he'd had as long as Adrian could remember.

Adrian's throat tightened. "Hi, Dad."

"You finally decided to visit."

"I…" He swallowed thickly. "I need your help."

"This have anything to do with that rogue shifter today?"

Adrian stiffened. "You know about that?"

"Randall keeps the shifters at the station up to date."

Of course. Wrangell-St. Elias bordered his parent's pack territory. Adrian just hadn't expected Randall to be in communication with his dad. But he shouldn't be surprised. The shifters who worked for the state were almost like a pack in and of themselves, regardless of their animal forms, and kept the shifter Council updated on shifter affairs.

But now wasn't the time for resentment or privacy. Adrian needed answers. "The rogue's not why I'm here."

"We just sat down to dinner." Dad pushed open the screen as he called over his shoulder, "Alice! Come see who's here."

Adrian remained frozen on the porch. He felt like he'd gone back in time ten years, a gangly fifteen-year-old waiting for Dad to punish him for ditching school or fighting. How was he supposed to confess he'd fucked up yet again? "I can't stay."

Mom's plump figure elbowed past Dad to fling her arms around Adrian's neck. "Adrian! We've been waiting for you forever."

Had she always been this tiny? He awkwardly patted her back. "Waiting for me? What do you mean?"

Behind his parents, Kepler appeared, his face unreadable. His brother wore ratty jeans and a black tee shirt that said RTFM. "We heard you were living in the park."

Guilt rose in Adrian's chest. As the two youngest, he and Kepler had been as close as litter mates growing up, and since returning to the area, Adrian had considered reaching out several times. But he never knew what to say, and then so much time passed, contacting Kepler only became more awkward.

Adrian nodded stiffly at Kepler. "Good to see you, man."

"Come, eat." Mom latched onto his hand, dragging him toward the dining room with the scarred wooden table he'd done his homework on as a kid. She pulled out his usual seat and turned to look at him all teary eyed. "I'm so glad you're here."

Adrian sat down while Mom set another plate in front of him, feeling off-balance under their unexpected welcome. She and Dad had sent him away. Hadn't wanted a mountain lion. Now they were acting as if he was a prodigal son.

"Why *are* you here?" Kepler sat in his place across the

table and crossed his arms. "You obviously want nothing to do with us."

Adrian looked his brother in the eyes. "I'm sorry I didn't call you, Kepler. But I wasn't welcome here."

Mom gasped. "Why would you say that?"

Adrian clenched both fists under the table, claws protruding against his palms. How could she not know? "You sent me to live with fucking lions!"

Mom's eyes were glassy with unshed tears. "You hated the pack. We only wanted to show you other options."

"I also talked to one of the bear Dens," Dad added. "But I thought you might prefer cats, even if they were the wrong kind. There weren't any mountain lions to foster you."

"We were struggling," Mom added. "You don't understand how many strings your dad pulled to keep you out of juvie."

How many times had he been suspended for fighting? Adrian had always been too willful and only followed instructions when they suited him. Only his years living among humans had forced him to take control of his aggression, which was easier if he stayed away from people. Even now, his instincts screamed at him to flee. *I'm not here to hash out my past.* He had more pressing problems. "I appreciate that. Really. But right now I need to know if there's a way to nullify a claiming mark."

Mom gasped, eyes brightening. "You found a mate?"

"Why would you want to annul a mark?" Dad's gray eyebrows furrowed.

Adrian sighed. "I made a mistake and I want to fix it."

"Why is it a mistake?"

"She's… not a shifter." The admission sent a flush of embarrassment through him.

Mom loaded his plate with casserole as if he was still a child. "Shifter or not, if your animal chose her, then she's the one. It's fate, Adrian. Are you worried she won't be a lion?"

"Mountain lion," Adrian corrected. He didn't want to answer questions, he just wanted a simple answer. But his family always talked things to death. Tried to convince him he was wrong. He wasn't wrong about this, and he didn't have time to argue. "I don't want her to become a shifter at all. I can't take a mate."

"You can't cut and run on a mate like you did with your family." Kepler sneered. "That shit's sacred."

"All right." Dad patted the air as if calming a puppy. "Let's just back up a minute. If your mountain lion chose her, why do you keep saying she's not your mate?"

"Having some needy female around all the time would drive me insane. I detest people. I can barely stand myself."

"Is she needy?" Dad asked.

Adrian realized he was misrepresenting Darcy. Sure, he'd helped her, but she wasn't what he'd call needy. He admired the way she was pursuing her witchcraft despite the coven's bullshit requirements. But he couldn't tell his family that. Bad enough he'd claimed a human; he didn't think he could face their judgment if they knew he'd claimed a witch.

He picked up his fork and pushed chunks of moose burger around his plate. "I'd just prefer to keep my space. I made a mistake."

Kepler glared across the table. "Ever consider your mistake might be running away? Again?"

His brother's words stung, but Adrian would make things up to him later, after he got through this mess with Darcy.

Mom put her hand on Adrian's arm. "Even mountain lions aren't meant to be alone all the time. Having a mate isn't about being social. It's about sharing common goals and putting someone else first. Give things a chance."

He pulled away from her touch and rose, pacing the small dining area as if it was a cage. He just wanted to go back to the way things were. But his mountain lion wanted to go back to Darcy's. Fuck, he needed to get her out of his head. "She doesn't want to be a shifter. I fucked up. I need to reverse the claim."

A knowing look infused Dad's face. "Is your problem that you don't want a mate, or is it that you want to protect this woman?"

Scowling, Adrian resumed his pacing. How the hell was he supposed to know? It felt as if he had a barbed hook in his heart. All it would take was a tug and Darcy'd pull him back to her side.

Dad followed Adrian's pacing with his eyes. "She doesn't have to become a shifter, but a claim can't be reversed, only replaced by another one."

Adrian's steps faltered, his claws and fangs straining to emerge. Even thinking about someone else with Darcy made his blood boil. He took shallow breaths, unable to form words as a growl rose from his throat.

"Listen, son," Dad continued. "You came here for my advice, so here it is. I say stick it out and give things a chance. She may surprise you. You may even surprise yourself."

Adrian stared at his feet, at the interlocking pattern of blue circles on the floor. He absently realized the linoleum was new, replaced since he'd been here last. Could he give things a chance with Darcy? He'd bitten her, changed her life forever. He rubbed his forehead. After the way he'd left, she might not even talk to him again.

"She doesn't have to become a shifter?" Adrian said it more to reassure himself than as a real question.

"If she doesn't drink from the Source, she'll stay as she is. The only thing that has changed is that you've bonded to her."

Kepler crossed his arms. "Adrian doesn't give a shit about bonds."

Meeting his brother's eyes, Adrian realized he'd done to Kepler exactly what he was now doing to Darcy. Abandoning someone important. Whether Darcy wanted him or not, he was bonded to her. He was part of her life. "All right. I'll give this a chance."

CHAPTER TWELVE

Eyes swollen from crying, Darcy rolled over in her bed and stared at the twilight sky outside her window. *He didn't even say thanks for the evening.* Granted, she didn't know Adrian well, but the way he'd left seemed out of place for the heroic man who'd risked his life for her and brought her gifts. Not all mates were fated, that much she knew, but for some reason, being with Adrian had felt special, not just an accident.

She shook her head violently back and forth over the pillow. If it wasn't for the ache between her legs and the tenderness on her shoulder, she might imagine Adrian had been a dream. A hot, primal, mind-blowing dream. But she needed to let it go. He obviously had.

The best way to stop thinking about Adrian was to stay busy, and she had plenty to do. She still needed to brew the potion for her upcoming apprenticeship test. She flung back the bedcovers and threw on some ratty sweatpants and a tee shirt.

In her kitchen, she brought out her mortar and pestle, the small propane burner she used for distillation, and several beakers and flasks. On her first attempt, the base elixir turned muddy instead of the clear gold it was supposed to be. She let out a shuddering breath. *Stay focused.* This had to be perfect—there was no room for mistakes. She dumped it, scrubbed everything, and started again.

Her second attempt overheated and cracked the beaker, spilling scalding liquid all over her countertop. She jumped back to avoid being splattered, sending her jar of pearl dust crashing to the floor. Fine white grit scattered across the linoleum, mixing with the ruined potion and bits of glass.

"Fuck fuck fuck!" She needed pearl dust for the potion.

A gagging odor rose from the mess, not unlike ozone and burning garbage. Goddess, her neighbors were going to report her for cooking meth or something. She raced to open the windows, letting in the cool morning breeze. Flinging open her front door, she gasped—Adrian sat on the stoop, knees drawn up, elbows resting on top of them.

He lifted his chin and looked at her. "Hey."

He came back!

He regarded her calmly, just as gorgeous in the pale dawn light as she remembered, all tawny-skinned and broad shouldered. Self-conscious, she glanced down at her disgusting sweat pants then back at him. "H-how long have you b-been out here?"

He rose as if pulled by magic strings, his golden eyes wild with determination that made her heart pound. "I didn't want to disturb you. May I take you to breakfast?"

The walls around her heart softened. He wanted to take her to breakfast? This was more like the Adrian she'd first invited to dinner. *Did he come up with a way to reverse the claim?* Her pulse felt like it was about to choke her, but she nodded. "I'll ch-change."

Wrinkling his nose, he peered past her into the apartment. "I'll wait out here."

Leaving the front door open, she swapped sweats for a teal green blouse with a high neckline that hid the bite on her shoulder and a matching peasant skirt, then followed Adrian to his pickup.

He opened the door for her like a gentleman, tucking her skirt against her legs after she climbed in, hand lingering a little longer than necessary at the back of her calf. Butterflies filled her stomach as his gaze traveled up her thigh and body to meet her eyes. "I seldom eat out. Where do you suggest we go?"

She directed him to a tiny café favored by locals. It was smaller than the lodge frequented by tourists, and she got the impression he'd prefer as little traffic as possible. And when they finished eating, the nearby apothecary would be open and she could purchase more pearl dust.

Morning light slanted through the café's windows across the four empty tables. An old man with barely three wisps of hair on his head sat near the café's register drinking coffee and reading a paper. A dark-haired waitress who looked like she was still wearing smudged eyeliner from a party last night looked up from wiping the counter. "Seat yourselves. I'll be there in a sec."

Adrian took her hand and led her to a booth table nearest the back exit. Such a little gesture shouldn't make her feel so happy, especially since he was about to tell her how to reverse his claim, but his touch made her smile. She sat, and he slid into the seat across from her, picking up the laminated menu. He perused it in silence while Darcy snuck glances at him over her own menu. Every time their eyes met, the butterflies in her stomach tried to take off. This was feeling less and less like a breakup breakfast. It almost felt like a date. *Is this a date?*

The waitress poured them coffee, and they both ordered sausage and cheese omelets. Darcy wasn't sure if she could eat, but coffee sounded great.

Adrian offered her the tiny pitcher of cream. "You take cream?"

"Thanks."

He poured a generous amount into her cup, then used the rest in his. Avoiding her gaze, he perused the menu again. He seemed as nervous as she was, and she found the idea endearing. Maybe this wasn't a breakup after all. Gaining confidence, she extended her leg until her foot met his beneath the table.

He lifted his chin, eyes flashing with unmistakable desire. Could this be the mating bond she'd been unable to find earlier? They barely knew each other, but her soul felt pulled to his. Normally, she wasn't much of a talker, but there was only one way to figure all this out.

She drew in a breath and asked, "Are we g-going to talk about last n-night?"

"I'm sorry, but there is no way to remove the claim."

Well, that was straightforward. She let out a shaky breath, surprised to discover she was less upset than she'd imagined she'd be. At least he'd come back and been honest with her.

He set his coffee down stoically. "Just so you know, I'm going to suck at this."

"At what?" She gulped out the words.

His gaze met hers. "A relationship."

Her heart skipped a beat. *He wants a relationship?* No one had ever said that to her before. She felt all warm and fuzzy inside. "Talking over breakfast is a g-good start."

"I like to be alone. A lot." He said it like he expected her to get up, brush her hands together, and walk away.

Thinking of how much time she spent alone studying to join the coven, she lifted one shoulder in a shrug. "I do, too."

"I'll probably piss you off and drive you away."

She got the feeling he'd been misunderstood much of his life, and it made him wary. He counteracted by striking first and running for cover. Sure, he'd hurt her feelings by leaving, but he'd come back, and she appreciated that. "I'm tenacious."

"I don't want to live in town." His voice rose at the end of his sentence, making it more of a question.

Now she understood. He was testing boundaries, sure he'd be rejected. "I'd never ask you t-to change, as l-long as you do the same for me."

A flicker of a smile crossed his face. "You have an answer for everything, don't you, kitten?"

She grinned, feeling giddy at the endearment. But then her grin faded. There was still the matter of the claiming. Had he done it by accident, or was there something special between them? If she was going to consider going forward with this, she needed to know. "Why did you bite me?"

He turned serious again. "My mountain lion thinks you're my mate."

A tingle ran up her spine. "Am I?"

A muscle in his jaw twitched and he tensed as if preparing to run, then he sandwiched her foot between both of his under the table. "Yes."

His eyes held uncertainty, as if he was waiting for her to deny him. All the awful things the coven members said about shifters played through her head. They were wrong. Adrian was sweet and strong and smart. She wanted to be with him. But she also wanted to be a witch. "I don't think I can be both a witch and a shifter. It's one magic or the other."

"You don't have to become a shifter if you don't want to. You can be whichever makes you most happy."

What if being his mate was her destiny? She felt closer to Adrian than she'd ever felt to anyone. He didn't finish her sentences for her or require small talk to feel engaged. And the sex—oh the sex!—couldn't possibly get better than it had been last night.

Then she thought about how her aunt would respond to this. "The c-coven looks d-down on shifters."

Feet withdrawing, he looked down at the coffee mug clenched in his hands. "I understand." He reached into his back pocket and retrieved his wallet. "Maybe your witches know a way to reverse my claim."

She stared at him, uncertain again. Would the witches know how to nullify the claim? Even if they did, did she want to give up a future with him? He might've run away at first, but then he'd come back for her, and that felt like it meant something. Why was he giving up so easily now? *He's trying to protect himself again.*

He dropped a couple of bills on the table. "If you ever need anything, let me know."

She grabbed his wrist before he could slide out of the booth. "Stop. W-we're in this together."

Before she could say more, the café door swung open and a gravelly voice cut through the quiet dining area. "That's the ranger."

A huge bearded man in a button-down plaid rumbled toward them like a freight engine, two other large men on his heels. They wove between the tables, oblivious to the shocked expression on the waitress's face, and stopped at the edge of the booth. The man glowered down at Adrian. "I recognize you. You're that punk from high school who got sent to juvie in Anchorage."

A muscle in Adrian's jaw bulged and his golden eyes narrowed, but he remained sitting. "You must be from the Den?"

"Damn straight, and we want answers."

Even Darcy could feel the challenge in his posture.

Adrian's hands remained clasped around his mug. "Happy to give them—at the inquest."

The man bent close to speak in Adrian's face. "You murdered my sister's mate, you bastard."

Darcy gasped as the man's canines flashed below his mustache. Now that she knew what to look for, she recognized a shifter's animal straining to get out. Was he a wolf? A bear? *Oh, Goddess.* She'd been attacked by a bear. "Th-the bear?"

The man's gaze flickered to her, upper lip curled to show more teeth. "Who are you?"

Her stomach leapt into her throat and she cringed against the padded seat.

Adrian rose. "Your issue's with me, not her. Now move along before someone calls the cops."

Stepping forward until he was nose to nose with Adrian, the man growled, "My sister has two cubs she has to raise on her own because of you." His nostrils widened. "You stink like ozone. Are you working for them?"

"Who?" she choked.

One of the other men put a meaty hand on his comrade's shoulder. "C'mon, Edric. This isn't the place for this."

Edric snarled and shrugged off the hand, never taking his eyes off Adrian. "You'll pay for what you did." He shot Darcy a scathing glance. "And your witch, too." Then he pivoted and strode out of the café, followed by his friends.

After a few beats of silence, the old man at the counter turned back to his paper, and the waitress brought them their food as if nothing had happened.

Darcy waited until the waitress moved out of earshot, then whispered, "That bear in the forest was a shifter?"

Adrian grimaced and rubbed his forehead. "A rogue."

"What's that?"

"Sometimes shifters lose control of their animal. Like going rabid." His brows drew together. "They have to be killed."

Tears pricked Darcy's eyes. That poor shifter. And poor Adrian for being forced to do the deed. Her insides still quaked from the malevolent glance the bearded man had given her before leaving. "Was he a shifter, too?"

"Yes. From the local grizzly den."

"Why did he think you're working for me?"

Adrian shook his head. "I'm not sure. My boss said there's some sort of rogue outbreak going on, maybe it has something to do with witches. The bear had unusual markings on it and smelled strange." He leaned back against the booth seat and tilted his head. "If witches are involved, it might be good to have you at the inquest with me."

Her throat constricted. "B-but I'm not a witch yet. I haven't passed the tests."

He cocked one eyebrow and leaned forward, covering her hand with his. "You will. Besides, you're an eyewitness."

She bit her lip. Going into a grizzly den sounded risky, especially if they were blaming witches. But she and Adrian were mates, and she'd better get used to being around other shifters. Besides, this was her chance to be there for Adrian, just like he'd been there for her.

Still mute, she nodded, hoping the shifters didn't expect her to do much talking.

CHAPTER THIRTEEN

*A*drian kept an eye on the door, wary that Edric might return with reinforcements. No one wanted to admit a family member had gone rogue. It was like admitting your loved one was a criminal on death row. Which it kind of was, since the only way to handle a rogue was to kill it.

Now Adrian was second guessing himself about asking Darcy to come to the inquest. If Edric was an example of what he'd face at the inquest, things could get violent, and Darcy didn't have a shifter form to protect herself. She didn't have accelerated healing like a shifter did. Hell, he didn't even know if her claiming mark was healing like it should.

Even dark thoughts couldn't extinguish his desire for her. She was only across the booth from him, yet felt too far away. Beneath the table, their feet still touched, a secret intimacy that made him yearn for more. He wanted to touch her everywhere. She was so fucking beautiful and shy. He loved that she didn't need to fill the silence with idle chatter, loved how he could be with her and still be able to breathe. *We're in this together.* For the first time in his life, he could actually picture spending the rest of his life with someone. *With her.*

She kept glancing at him beneath her lashes as they ate. Another couple entered the café, and the gentle buzz of conversation and clinking dishes grew louder. Adrian's mountain lion itched to get away, but then his gaze would connect with Darcy's and the beast inside him would calm, as if her presence was a shield.

Darcy polished off her omelet with surprising thoroughness and nodded gratefully at the waitress when she filled their coffees again. Just like him, she enjoyed a healthy dollop of cream in her brew, and she shared a look with him over the rim of her cup as they both sipped. His gaze dropped to her shoulder. "How's your mark?"

She pulled aside the collar of her shirt, craning her head to look at the scab. "It will heal."

Voice thick, he said, "I'm sorry I hurt you."

Her fingertips traced his claim, and her eyelids

fluttered as if the sensation surprised her. "It doesn't hurt. Actually, the opposite…"

Her gaze returned to his, eyes dark with her arousal, and he couldn't help smirking. If that didn't prove they were mates, he didn't know what would. He looked forward to showing her just how arousing a claiming mark could be.

The waitress cleared their dishes and Darcy glanced at her phone. "Darn."

"What is it?"

"I need to stop at the apothecary shop, b-but it doesn't open for another hour."

He realized that with breakfast over, the date was coming to an end, and he wasn't ready to let her go. "We could take a walk until then."

Her face lit up, and she nodded. As they rose from the booth, she took his hand. The casual affection felt good. *Right.* He never would've believed he might crave another person's company this much.

He allowed her to lead him from the café through the parking lot to the dirt road fronting the building. Although he could hear traffic on the two-lane highway from here, the dirt road they walked along remained blessedly empty. Side by side, they strolled toward a gray wooden sign in the ditch several hundred feet away. As they drew closer, he read *Hazel's Tea and Herbs* in white, hand-painted lettering with an arrow pointing toward a driveway.

Darcy paused and pointed, "That's the apothecary." She leaned close and gave him an exaggerated wink. "Don't tell anyone, but the owner's a witch."

He smiled back, breathing her in, thinking more about the way her hand felt in his than the witch at the end of the driveway. Running his thumb along the edge of her palm, he imagined other soft skin he'd like to be touching. If she hadn't expressed a need to visit the apothecary, he'd have swept her back to her place to get naked again. As it was, his pants felt too tight as they continued walking.

They chatted about growing up, realizing they'd both been in Anchorage at the same time while in high school. But where he'd been a troubled homeless teen, she'd been living in a very nice house on the Hillside with her mom. "How'd your mom die?" he asked softly.

"C-car accident." She shrugged one shoulder, eyes sad. "I've come to terms with it, and Aunt Willow took me in. Why were you homeless in Anchorage? I thought you said you have family in the area."

He put his arm around her waist so they walked hip to hip. Although he had to take shorter strides to match hers, she fit against him perfectly. "Mom and Dad didn't know what to do with a teenage mountain lion. Especially one that kept causing trouble."

He explained to her how they thought he needed fostering with other lions and how mountain lions weren't much like savannah lions. Although he hated to admit it, after his recent visit to his parent's house, he was beginning to think he'd been wrong about their intentions. "They were as confused as I was. If it hadn't been for Mr. Wombly, I'd probably be dead now. He was an old black bear shifter at my school. He made sure I had food and clothes, got me through school, and eventually pulled some strings to get me a job here."

"Right b-back where you started." She nodded as if it made perfect sense.

"Huh, you're right." Now that he looked back, he almost wondered if Mr. Wombly had been in touch with his parents the whole time. He'd have to ask when he saw them again. But he didn't want to think about that now.

Stopping at the side of the road near some large aspen trees, he pulled her against him. "I can't take it anymore."

She lifted her chin, mouth parted in what he believed was an invitation. Lowering his head, he kept his gaze locked with hers until their lips met. She responded warmly, sliding both arms around his waist to press herself against him. He kissed her, his fingers threading into her silken hair at the base of her neck. She was so fucking intoxicating.

He walked her backward between the trees, supporting her from stumbling until her back met the smooth bark of a trunk. Taking a wide stance in front of her, his erection felt like a living thing, surging toward her, fighting the constraints of his clothing. Her kisses were as fevered as his as she tilted her head back against the trunk.

Sweet tea and flowers and luscious female filled his senses, and he devoured her mouth in long, sure strokes of his tongue. Her hands slipped around behind him to cup his ass, grinding herself against his hard cock. She lifted one leg, the heat of her sex warm as she opened to him, and he dry-pumped her against the trunk, eliciting a soft moan from her. God, this was bliss.

He kissed along her jaw, nibbled her earlobe, brushed his mouth over her shoulder where her shirt hid his claiming mark.

She gasped, nipples hardening against his chest. "W-why is that so sensitive?"

"It's a reinforcement of the bond."

"Will it always feel like this?" She tilted her head, exposing her throat.

"Yes," he growled, loving how she yielded to him. Whether or not she ever became a shifter and gave him a mark didn't matter. She was his, and he would cherish her for as long as she would allow it. But now wasn't the time to bite her. He satisfied himself by setting his blunt teeth lightly over her fabric-covered mark.

She cried out and bucked against him. He inserted one hand between them, lifting her skirt to find the hot dampness between her thighs. "So sexy," he murmured against her shoulder as he slipped his fingers beneath her panties and into her slick folds. Dipping into her, he drew her juices up to circle her clit. Over and over he teased her while she matched his rhythm, her fingers clawing into his shoulders.

A car drove past without slowing, kicking up a cloud of dust, but he didn't pause. She was making tiny mewling gasps, obviously trying to be quiet as he brought her toward climax. When she let out a strangled noise and shuddered, he shifted his hand from behind her head to her waist, holding her up as her supporting leg threatened to give out. He wrung every last ripple of sensation from her until she sagged against him, breathing hard.

He held her, his cheek on top of her hair, his nose filled with her scent. "You are amazing," he mumbled, cock still aching, but soul satisfied.

"I th-thought mates are supposed to be able to hear each other's thoughts."

"I think you have to claim me back for that to happen. You need your animal to do that."

She lifted her chin to meet his gaze. "So I can't claim you if I'm a witch?"

He kissed the tip of her nose. "It doesn't matter. As long as you accept my claim, we're bonded."

They were bonded, soul to soul, and whether or not she was a shifter mattered as little as the color of her skin or eyes.

A naughty twinkle filled her gaze, and she dropped one hand from his shoulder to cover his erection. "I have another way to claim you."

He groaned and closed his eyes, the pressure of her hand making him want to burst. She unfastened his belt and flicked open the button of his fly. His engorged cock almost undid the zipper on its own, straining to be free, and she had him in hand within moments.

She threw her leg up over his hip, shoving aside the crotch of her panties and guiding him to her entrance. He pumped forward, impaling her hot folds in a single thrust. She moaned, hips straining to meet his. He wrapped both hands around her ass, lifting her to seat himself more fully inside her. He pressed her against the tree trunk, body hard against her softness as he reveled in her tight heat around him. Damn, she felt so good.

He rocked back, then plunged forward again while she looked fiercely into his eyes. Slowly his rhythm built until he was pistoning into her, his hands crushed between the bark and her ass, but he didn't care. He drove forward with relentless intensity, her heels locked behind his hips. The pressure in his balls rose to intolerable heights.

She threw her head back, mouth open in a choked moan as her inner walls tightened around him. Her orgasm was his undoing. He tipped over the edge, cock pulsing and jetting deep into her core. She took all of him, her orgasm milking every last drop while he held her tight, riding out the shuddering waves of pleasure.

After his breathing slowed, he pulled away from the tree, letting her slide down off him and back to her feet. She wobbled, hands on his shoulders to steady herself. He smoothed a damp strand of hair off her flushed cheek. Her eyes widened, and she grabbed his wrist to look at the backs of his hands, scraped raw from being up against the bark. "You're hurt."

"I'll be fine. Shifters heal fast." Another car drove past, a blur of color between the tree trunks, and he closed his fly. "I'm sorry. Seducing you on the side of the road isn't what I'd call a good second date."

She shook her head and rose to her toes to kiss him on the mouth. "Technically, I'd still call this our f-first date. But who's counting?"

He smiled with genuine affection. Hard to believe they'd only just met yesterday. He'd never been this happy. Fate had definitely picked this woman for him. Lacing his fingers with hers, he said, "Let's get you to the apothecary shop and finish your potion."

CHAPTER FOURTEEN

*D*arcy's heartbeat felt like it might never slow down again. She'd never been into risk taking, but the thrill of doing something like that in public sang through her blood. As if the thrill of being with Adrian wasn't enough already. The coven insisted shifters were barely more than beasts, but he could be as gentle as he was forceful. He'd kept his hands between her and the tree trunk, and she knew he'd wanted to bite her again, but he hadn't.

She leaned her cheek against his shoulder as they walked. He felt so good. Smelled so good. Goddess, she'd wanted to bite him back there. To put her mark on him and let the entire world know that he was hers and she was his and nothing could change that. But she couldn't do that without becoming a shifter, and she'd worked too hard to become a witch to give up now.

They reached the apothecary shop just as Hazel, the owner, was flipping the sign on the front door to OPEN. The single story log cabin looked as if it had been here since the Gold Rush, but was well-maintained, with marigolds in the flower boxes at the tiny windows and wildflowers growing from the sod-covered roof.

Hazel smiled and pushed open the door when she spotted Darcy. "Good morning, Darcy. You're out early."

"M-morning, Hazel." Darcy felt her voice shrinking, even though Hazel had never been anything but kind to her. "I need p-pearl dust, please."

"Of course." Hazel gave Adrian a curious glance but didn't linger, heading into the store.

Earthy, herb-scented air rushed over Darcy as she led Adrian inside, moving past shelves overflowing with books, glass jars, teacups and teapots, mortars and pestles. A few exquisitely woven grass baskets sat next to a pair of hand-sewn mukluks in a case that also held semi-precious crystals and jewelry made by a local artist.

Adrian paced slightly behind her, cautiously looking at everything they passed. She squeezed his hand in assurance. "This'll only t-take a sec."

The back corner of the store held a huge cabinet with shelves and drawers, the area sectioned off by a wooden workbench and some thick rope. From the rope hung a piece of paper that said, *Please Ask For Assistance*. Hazel stepped over the rope and opened one of the cabinet doors, pulling down a scale and a glass jar.

A scrawny husky mix with one blue eye and one hazel eye poked its head around the counter. Darcy held out her hand to the dog. "Hi, J-jake." Jake was Hazel's familiar, but he'd always seemed like a plain old friendly dog to Darcy. He even liked belly scratches and the occasional liver treat. Suddenly, his tail went down and his ears laid back. He barked once, sharply.

Hazel's smile tightened as her gaze moved from her dog to Adrian and Darcy's clasped hands then up to Adrian's face. "Shifter, huh? I don't see many of you in here." She measured pearl dust into a small brown bottle. "Making something special?"

Darcy shrugged, for some reason feeling as though Hazel'd caught them having sex in the alley. "Just something t-to help me with my test tomorrow."

"Ah," Hazel nodded, uncertainty still in her eyes, and handed Darcy the bottle. "Your aunt mentioned you're trying to join the coven. You don't need to join one to be a witch, you know."

Aunt Willow insisted respectable witches had covens, but Darcy would never say that to Hazel. She'd heard that Hazel'd had a falling out with hers. *Like my mom.* She wondered why, but it would be rude to ask, so she just nodded. "Th-thank you."

After paying for the dust, Adrian drove her home, taking her through the neighborhood where he'd grown up and pointing out his old school, his parents' house, and places he'd played as a child. The last time he'd mentioned his family, he'd seemed resentful, but now he seemed less bitter. She wondered what had changed. "Your family sounds nice."

He pursed his lips and nodded. "They're not be as bad as I once thought."

She took his hand into her lap and stroked the back of it. "Can I meet them?"

Turning his palm up, he grasped her fingers and shot her a smile. "Someday. I have a few issues to work out first."

Did Adrian worry about introducing a witch as his mate? Aunt Willow came to mind, and she wondered how the witch would react to meeting Adrian. *Not well.* Shifters and witches did not mingle, let alone mate. She decided to drop the matter until they'd both had time to adjust.

He walked her to her door, and she was relieved to find the terrible smell from her botched potion had dissipated. She turned to him shyly. She really should start working, but she wasn't ready for him to leave. "W-would you like to come in?"

He feathered his fingers along her cheek and kissed her nose, her mouth, then pressed his forehead to hers. "I'd love to. But I have to go to work, and I know you need to make your potion." His voice was huskier than usual as he added, "I had a great time with you this morning."

"I d-did, too." She wrapped both arms around his waist and hugged him tight. "Can I see you later tonight?"

He hugged her back. "Yes. How about we actually eat those steaks tonight? I'll be back after I do some paperwork for my boss."

She realized she was grinning like an idiot against his chest. *He wants to come back.*

He kissed the top of her head and put his hands on her shoulders to push her upright. "Now go get that potion made so the rest of the night can be mine. I have naughty plans for you."

Tingles jetted through her at his promise. She nodded and held up crossed fingers. "Wish me luck."

His eyes crinkled, and he wrapped his hand around her

crossed fingers, bringing them to his mouth to kiss the tips. "You got this. Third time's the charm, right?"

She nodded and watched him trot down the stairs back to his waiting pickup. Floating on air and full of confidence, she returned to her apartment and assembled her ingredients, absolutely certain he was right.

CHAPTER FIFTEEN

$\mathcal{A}$drian drove back to his cabin as if in a dream. His mountain lion was happy. He was happy. He couldn't imagine things being any better. Darcy helped make him feel like he belonged.

He drove up the steep, winding dirt road, glancing at the gorgeous view that opened up on his left. He'd never really appreciated how pretty the land in the park was. He returned his eyes to the road, thinking of his run-down cabin. He should fix it up, maybe buy some new furniture. The house had no plumbing, but he could look into fixing that. Maybe an outdoor bath house. He could clear a few trees and put it where it looked directly out on this amazing view. Once he'd checked in with Randall, he'd head back to town and order lumber.

He pulled up to the cabin and frowned. A white pickup was parked outside. In the shadows of his screened porch, a bulky figure sat on his rickety chair. Adrian cut the engine and got out, stopping about ten feet from the base of the steps. *Edric.* The brawny bear shifter's cold eyes regarded Adrian as if the ranger was the one intruding.

"What're you doing here?"

"Gathering evidence." The chair creaked as the shifter rose to his feet.

The hairs on the back of Adrian's neck prickled, and he turned. Edric's cohorts had surrounded him from behind. They were still in human form, but his thighs tensed as his mountain lion surged inside him, demanding to be let free. Ready to brawl. He kept his shift in check. Three grizzlies wasn't a fight he could win, and they'd be on him before he could shift and run. *I should've been more cautious.*

He crossed his arms, mostly to try to hold in his mountain lion, and turned back to Edric. *Remain calm. Do your job.* The Den had the right to inspect the scene. The rank stink of the three bear shifters made Adrian want to sneeze. "I'll take you to the site."

"Already been there." Edric clunked slowly down the wooden porch steps. "I'm thinking maybe you're the one gone rogue. You got no Den, Pride, or Pack to keep you in check. Living up here all alone, it'd be easy to go a little crazy. You took it out on my brother-in-law."

Adrian's spine stiffened. Being accused of going rogue was a serious threat. And Edric was right, Adrian had no one to back him up if the inquisition turned that direction. No Alpha to vouch for him. Not even Randall's testimony would carry much weight. "I'm a mountain lion, not a fucking pack animal. We're designed to be alone."

Edric sneered. "Where's your witch, pussycat?"

Adrian edged sideways and bared his teeth at both the insult and the threat. Darcy couldn't be dragged into this mess. These bears were looking for a scapegoat. Perhaps it had been a mistake asking her to the inquest. "I told you, keep her out of this."

Footsteps behind Adrian let him know the other two were keeping pace with his movement, flanking him. *Fuck.* What the hell did they want?

Edric lowered his chin, eyes flashing. As if that was a signal, four hands grappled Adrian's biceps. He thrashed, twisting and snarling, but it was three against one. Edric landed a hard fist into Adrian's stomach, doubling him over. Damn bears could pack a punch. Sucking in a breath, he straightened and threw his head back, aiming for the nose of the man on his left. The man dodged, but unbalanced enough to allow

Adrian to lash out at Edric with a foot. The big man grunted and clutched his groin.

"Fucking lion hits below the belt," one of the men said, jerking Adrian's arm up painfully behind him.

Something hard cinched around his wrist, and the next thing he knew, they bound his hands. He struggled, knowing it was futile. "You have no right to restrain me."

Huffing, Edric straightened. He looked a little green around the gills, but it hadn't diminished his fury. He grabbed Adrian by the throat and brought his face close. "You'll pay, little pussy. Believe me, you'll pay."

Adrian choked for breath, stars pressing the edges of his vision. And then the world went dark.

CHAPTER SIXTEEN

$\mathcal{D}$arcy held her breath as she squeezed a single drop of *Populus tremuloides* syrup into the thumb-sized vial. The sparkling gold elixir brightened and a scent similar to wintergreen wafted toward her. She stared a moment longer, waiting for something to go wrong. The potion continued swirling, unchanged.

"I did it," she breathed.

Corking the vial, she wrapped it in velvet and placed it in one of the inner pockets of her purse. For a few long moments, she stared at her handbag, as if she might wake up from a dream at any moment. But her eyes were grainy and tired, her hands sore from using the mortar and pestle, and her shoulder still ached a little from Adrian's bite.

She was not dreaming.

This was the best day of her life.

She lifted her arms, threw back her head, and twirled across her living room to a song only in her head. *A witch, a witch, I'll prove I'm a witch!*

Collapsing backward onto her sofa, she thought of how pleased Aunt Willow would be when she aced the incantation tests. A small pang seized her heart as she remembered how her mother'd insisted she'd never have the talent and shouldn't even try. She shoved the thought aside. *Focus on success.*

Closing her eyes, she envisioned herself as a coven apprentice. The image flitted out of her grasp. She was so *tired*. Even the eloquence potion wouldn't do much good if she fell asleep over the spells. She cracked open one eye and looked at the sky outside her front window. Evening was still a few hours away. She should take a quick nap before Adrian returned. She'd barely shut her eyes before she sank into blissful slumber.

When she woke, twilight bathed her living room in purple half-light. She sat bolt upright. *What time is it?* It didn't get dark this time of year until around midnight. She rose and stumbled to the kitchen, coming to a full stop when she saw the time on the microwave clock. *Two?* As in two a.m.? She retrieved her phone from the kitchen table, double checking. The time was correct. Had she missed Adrian? There were no missed calls on her phone, no texts. She hurried to her front door and flung it open, hoping to find him waiting there.

No Adrian.

Where was he? Had she misunderstood how late he'd be? *Or maybe he changed his mind.* She slowly closed the door and stood staring at it in confusion. Then she grabbed her phone and dialed the number he'd programmed into it over breakfast. It went to a generic voicemail. Doubt lanced through her. Was it really his number? "H-hi, Adrian. It's D-Darcy." She gulped, trying to control her stutter. "I hope you're all right. Please call when you get this."

She hung up and stared at the screen, hoping he might dial back immediately. When he didn't, she tucked her phone into her back pocket and began cleaning up her kitchen. By three-thirty, he still hadn't called or shown up. She dialed again, but didn't leave another message. Her gut churned. Something was wrong. Their connection was real. No way had he stood her up. If only she could talk to him in her head.

He'd said he lived in a cabin near the trailhead. It shouldn't be hard to find. Taking a quick shower, she dressed and grabbed her purse and keys. When she pulled into the ranger's cabin, she breathed a sigh of relief. His truck was here.

She got out and rushed to the front door. No one answered her knock, and when she tried the handle, the door swung open. "Adrian?"

No answer. She stepped inside, glancing around the small front room. He wasn't here, and the back room with its king-sized bed was empty, too. She hurried back outside, calling his name. Where could he be?

This had to have something to do with that shifter in the café this morning. She didn't know how to reach the bear shifters, but she did know where Adrian's parents lived. Perhaps they would know.

The sun was rising when she reached the long driveway with the overflowing nasturtium planters and a State Trooper's car in the driveway that Adrian had showed her earlier. *Goddess, it's fucking early to knock on someone's door.* But what choice did she have? If the bears had decided to take revenge on Adrian, every second counted. She took a deep breath and jabbed her index finger against the doorbell.

After a long few minutes she heard footsteps inside. The door flung open to reveal an older man with short gray hair wearing a white tee shirt and boxers. He rubbed his eyes. "Are you in trouble, Miss?"

She swallowed, mouth gone dry. "I-I-I'm l-l-look-looking for Adrian."

The man straightened and his grizzled eyebrows drew together. "He doesn't live here anymore. Who, may I ask, are you?"

Barely able to catch her breath, she managed to squeak out, "His m-mate."

His expression changed to understanding, and he pushed open the screen door. "Please, come in."

Darcy took half a step back, shaking her head. "I d-don't mean to bother you. I just need to know how to reach the bear shifters."

"Why do you need to talk to them?"

She stammered out the story of the shifter in the café. "Adrian w-was supposed to come to my house for dinner. And he's n-not answering his phone."

Another male voice rose from somewhere behind the older man. "You're certain he didn't just run away?"

The older man looked over his shoulder as a guy about Adrian's age came into view. His torso was just as ripped as Adrian's and there was a similarity to the shape of his nose and eyebrows. Definitely Adrian's brother.

Darcy shook her head. "He w-wouldn't do that."

Adrian's dad scratched his stubbled cheek, looking thoughtful. "I suppose it can't hurt to call the Den and see if they know anything." He gestured for her to come in. "You're welcome to wait inside while I do. I'm Kyle, by the way, Adrian's father."

"D-Darcy." Pulse thundering in her ears, Darcy stepped inside.

The screen door banged closed behind her, and Adrian's dad retreated down a hallway. The living room was small, with a fireplace on the far wall flanked by a well-worn recliner. A sofa and matching love seat sat opposite each other. *I'm in a shifter's home.* A wolf pack, she thought, eyeing the younger man.

He looked her up and down. "Coffee?"

She nodded, not trusting her voice.

He pointed with his chin toward the afghan-covered couch near the front window. "Have a seat. I'm Kepler."

"Hi," she managed as she moved to the couch.

Left alone, she listened to low mumbling from down the hall where Adrian's dad had gone. A drip coffeemaker gurgled from the kitchen, followed by the rich scent of dark roast. After a few minutes, a woman in a bathrobe emerged from the back where Adrian's dad had gone. Her dusty blonde hair was mussed, her face lined with worry. She offered a hand. "I'm Alice, Adrian's mother. What's your name, dear?"

"Darcy B-blackwell."

"Good to meet you, Darcy. It turns out Adrian is at the Den." Her already concerned face grew tighter. "He has a meeting with them this morning."

"T-today?" Why would Adrian schedule the inquest without telling her? She got the sickening feeling things had gone terribly wrong. "He wanted me at the meeting, too."

"Of course," Alice said. "His mate should be there."

Adrian's dad returned from the back, this time fully dressed in a State Trooper's uniform at the same moment Kepler returned with two mugs of coffee. The younger man shot a curious look at his father and handed him a mug before carrying the other to Darcy. "Adrian's in trouble again?"

Kyle hooked a thumb over his shoulder. "Both of you get dressed. We need to get to the Den immediately."

A strange feeling rippled the air, almost like a scent Darcy couldn't quite place, and Kepler and Alice hurried away. Sipping his coffee, Kyle paced in front of Darcy. "I don't know if I can get him out of this one."

She kept her fingers wrapped around her mug, even though it was scalding her fingers. "Th-this one?"

"My son had a reputation as a troublemaker growing up. The Den thinks he's gone rogue."

Adrian's description of rogues went through her mind. *They have to be killed.* She shot to her feet, sloshing hot coffee over her hands. "No!"

"He said you're his mate." He paused his pacing and took a deep breath. "But you don't smell like a shifter. Or a human. What are you?"

"I'm a witch." She braced herself, uncertain how he'd respond.

He rubbed his forehead with his fingertips. "He didn't mention that. This complicates things."

"How?"

"There are rumors there's a witch behind the rogue infection." He met her gaze, eyes filled with worry. "It might be better if you don't come to the inquest."

"But I'm an eyewitness. The b-bear attacked me."

He frowned. "They'll assume you're lying."

"What happens if they find him g-guilty?"

Kyle's gaze slid away. "There's no such thing as shifter prison."

In other words, they'd kill him. And it sounded like the odds were against him. Darcy might be a witch, but she was Adrian's mate, and his only eye witness. *Your testimony's no good if they don't believe you.* Her gaze fell to her purse lying on the sofa. *The eloquence potion.* It would allow her to perform the coven's incantations without stuttering tonight—or she could use it to make her testimony for Adrian infallible.

She set her coffee on the end table and shouldered her purse. "I'm c-coming."

drian licked blood from his lip and looked out over the assembled crowd of shifters. The back room of the bar the Den used for meetings was standing room only. He was honestly a little surprised to be here alive. He'd been certain Edric and the boys had intended to take him to the middle of nowhere and kill him. But after roughing him up and trying in vain to torture a confession out of him, Edric said he wanted his sister to have the satisfaction of seeing Adrian's face when he died.

Now, handcuffed to a heavy wooden chair, Adrian faced a host of at least thirty shifters, mostly bears, but including a smattering of wolves and one moose who worked at the Forest Service. The dead shifter's widow and two small children sat front and center. The poor woman's eyes were swollen and red, and one little boy lay on her lap while the other clutched her hand. Adrian's heart went out to them, but his mountain lion was clawing to escape the choking musk of the Den.

The dead shifter lay in a huge casket not fifteen feet from him, muzzle pointed toward the ceiling, front claws crossed over its belly as if it were a human. He'd never been to a funeral for a shifter in animal form before, but the sight was eerie as fuck. Between Adrian and the casket, the Den's Grayback stood at a podium. Adrian had already given his description of the event, leaving Darcy's name out of things by saying he'd come upon a hiker under attack, and by the time the fight was over, the hiker had fled.

The Grayback called Randall to the stand.

Randall took a seat at the front, facing the room. The werewolf had dressed in a dark blue suit, his light brown hair neatly parted and cheeks cleanly shaven. He frowned at Adrian's disheveled clothing and bloodied lip. Adrian shrugged. It wasn't as if Edric had given him a chance to make himself presentable.

The Grayback pounded his gavel to silence the murmuring crowd. "Please state your name and relationship to the accused for the record."

"Randall McIntyre. I'm Adrian's supervisor with the Forest Service."

"And what do you know about the murder of the bear shifter, Wilson Rhodes."

"I wouldn't call it murder. Adrian reported a rogue shifter had been killing and abandoning animals within the park's boundaries. Between the local news taking an interest and the recent increase in rogue activity, I felt we needed to get ahead of the situation, so I gave him the go-ahead to exterminate it."

The crowd buzzed loudly, and the Grayback banged his gavel against the podium. "What proof did he provide that this was the shifter that had been killing animals?"

"He said there were bear tracks around the sites, and he smelled it."

"Do you have any of this in your reports?"

Randall glanced at Adrian. "Not evidence about this bear, specifically."

Adrian's stomach churned. Randall had always been on him about filing reports, taking photos, creating a paper trail.

The Grayback cleared his throat. "Is it possible the accused was making the kills himself and looking for another shifter to blame?

Randal shook his head. "I've known Adrian over a year

now, and I've never seen any indication of him losing control of his animal."

"Answer the question, please. Yes or no."

"Well, I suppose, yes, but that's pretty far-fetched if you ask me."

"Do you know why the accused attacked Wilson in his animal form?"

"My ranger said he came upon the bear attacking a hiker."

The Grayback nodded once. "Thank you, that will be all."

People at the back of the room rumbled as Randall returned to his seat. Adrian didn't like the worried lines on his supervisor's face, but he was glad to have Randall here. If nothing else, the werewolf could tell Adrian's family what had happened. *And Darcy.* Adrian's heart ached thinking of her. She might never know what happened to him if this played out the way he expected. But at least he'd kept her name out of things. She'd be safe from shifter retribution.

The widow took the stand, describing her mate as stable and loving. Following her, a line of bears vouched for Wilson's stability. The Grayback tapped his gavel and looked down at Adrian. "That concludes the assessment of the deceased's character. Do you have anyone else to speak on your behalf, Adrian Stone?"

Before Adrian could even shake his head, a woman's voice rose from the back of the room. "I'll represent him."

Darcy? His heart fell. How did she find the Den? Now they'd know who she was. The throng of shifters parted, allowing Darcy to step forward. Behind her, his parents, Kepler, and even his older brother Jonas followed.

Growls filled the room, and Edric jumped from his seat. "It's the witch he was with at the café!"

"Order!" The Grayback cracked his gavel.

Darcy's gaze remained steady on Adrian as she advanced, head held high as she passed rows of bristling shifters. Flashes of fur and fangs appeared in the crowd, but she didn't bat an eye. Even without an animal to call on, she was ferocious, and damned beautiful.

"Who are you?" The Grayback asked.

"I'm his mate." She turned to face the room. "And I'm the hiker Wilson attacked."

A collective gasp filled the room.

"She's lying." Edric stalked forward. "This is the witch I mentioned. She's probably the one turning shifters rogue."

"Stay the fuck away from my mate," Adrian snarled, struggling against the cuffs binding him to his chair. His mountain lion was right at the surface, fighting to break free, but if he shifted now, he'd only prove he was unstable.

"Edric, sit down or I'll have you removed," the Grayback ordered. He turned to Darcy. "Miss, this is a shifter matter. Witches have no business here."

Darcy pulled the collar of her blouse down, revealing the scabbed claiming mark on her pale freckled skin. "I may not be a shifter, but Adrian claimed me, and that means by shifter law, I can speak for him."

Adrian frowned. There was something different about her. Not just her sudden knowledge about shifter law, but a glow, an eloquence that made her words ring true. And she smelled like ozone. *She isn't stuttering*, he realized.

The widow rose, tears streaming down her cheeks. "My Wilson would never kill for sport, let alone attack a hiker. You must've provoked him."

"Those white patches on his fur weren't there before he took that witch's job," Edric added. "He was hexed, I'm certain."

Darcy faced the widow, her eyes tight with sympathy. "My deepest condolences for your mate. I understand the loss you're feeling right now. However, I assure you, I had no interaction with your mate prior to his attack. Adrian only stepped in to protect me. If he hadn't, I'd be dead right now, and you would be holding a different kind of meeting, possibly with a lot of press. Adrian's quick action spared shifter kind from discovery by humans. You should be giving him an award, not abusing him and threatening his life."

The audience mumbled, and Adrian felt the animosity in the room shrink. To his surprise, several onlookers bobbed their heads in agreement. A flush crept into his face. He was not used to attention of any kind. It was one thing for Darcy to defend him, but she couldn't possibly think she could turn him into a hero. She glanced his way, and the moment of shared contact let him know that's exactly what she was doing.

Darcy was on fire, not only in the steadiness of her voice, but the set of her shoulders as she faced the room. "My mate has full control of his animal, which I'm certain he's already proven by the look of him." Darcy focused on Edric. "Did he lose control while you were beating him?"

The big man sat with his arms crossed, face a deep red-purple. His eyes flashed with the power of his animal, but he shook his head no.

The Grayback said, "Please respond out loud. Did the accused at any point lose control of his animal during his capture or interrogation?"

"No," Edric rumbled.

"Thank you for your honesty," Darcy said, moving to Adrian's side and addressing the Grayback. "I know I'm new to your community, and I'm not even a shifter. But I am his mate. I know him to the bottom of his soul. As such, I vouch for him, and I respectfully request you release him immediately."

"We vouch for him, as well," Dad said from where he still stood in the audience, followed by the rest of his family's agreement.

The Grayback rubbed his nose, looking from Adrian to Darcy. "You smell strange for a witch, I'll admit. But as his mate, your testimony will be considered. Let the Den council make their judgement."

After a few moments of muttering, a tall woman with wildly curly black hair stood. "We find the extermination of Wilson Rhodes to have been lawfully executed."

The audience rumbled, some in agreement, others with arguments. The Grayback said, "Release the accused." He leveled a look at Edric. "And let no one set paw upon him out of turn, or face the full punishment of the Den. Am I understood?"

Edric mumbled, "Yes, Alpha."

One of the bears released Adrian's cuffs, and he rose, gathering Darcy in his arms and crushing her hard against him. She squeezed him back just as fiercely.

He looked up to find his family approaching. His father patted him on the back, and Kepler was nodding and grinning as he surveyed Adrian's arms around his mate. "Well done, bro."

Adrian looked down at his mate. "No, well done, Darcy."

She flushed and beamed. "I love you."

"I love you, too. Now let's go home."

CHAPTER EIGHTEEN

Darcy kept hold of Adrian's hand as they exited the bar, taking him to her car and depositing him in the passenger seat. She knew he'd said shifters healed fast, but he honestly looked like shit, and she wanted to clean him up and make sure he was all right. His parents and brothers stayed behind to keep an eye on the bears, just in case they changed their minds, but she didn't think that would be a problem. Her eloquence potion had worked like a charm.

"What happened to your stutter?" Adrian asked as she started the engine. Goddess, his voice sounded as ragged as he looked.

She pulled into the street and headed toward her house. "I took the eloquence potion."

"It worked? That's great!" He leaned back against the headrest, then jerked upright again. "Wait, you said it was temporary. What about your test?"

She shook her head. She'd thought about that a lot on the drive to the Den. "I'm dropping my application."

He turned to look at her. "I don't understand. Passing that test means everything to you."

"Not everything." She shot him a smile. "I realized I wanted to join the coven to please my aunt. To make up for whatever my mom did to upset her. And now I'm mated to a shifter—which I wouldn't change for the world—and the coven will never accept that." She turned on her signal as she slowed for the turn off the highway. "Why would I want to belong to a group that can't accept me as I am?"

"But how are you going to learn witchcraft?"

"I don't need a coven to study magic. Hazel isn't with a coven. And I m-made that potion all by myself." She swallowed, feeling the potion's effects fading. Gripping the steering wheel, she kept talking, wanting to get it all out before her speech went back to normal. "You've shown me that I don't need a coven to be whole. I only need to be sure of myself. The same way you're sure of yourself. You make me feel strong. Capable. And I love your family. I know there were some problems between you guys, but they came through when it counted."

He chuckled. "Whoa, that's a lot of words, kitten. Slow down and take a breath."

She pulled into her driveway, knowing he was poking fun to hide his fears. It's what he did. But she would not let him off so easily. Before Adrian, she'd been alone, an outsider looking for a way in. She'd believed she wasn't worthy. He gave her confidence just by looking at her, by giving her space to form her own words and opinions. Because of him, she'd discovered the best and strongest part of herself. "I love you, Adrian. I don't need a coven because I have a family— you. And nothing else matters but you."

He looked into her eyes, Adam's apple bobbing with a swallow. Reaching behind her neck, he leaned in close until their foreheads touched. "I love you, too, Darcy. I'll join a pack if that makes you happy."

"I don't need you to join a pack. I just want you to be friendly when you can and n-not be afraid to ask for help."

He nodded. "That I can do."

Knowing the time for words was over, she kissed him with everything she had and then some.

unt Willow was displeased with Darcy's decision, to put it mildly. They sat across from each other in the café. "I pulled a lot of strings to get you this interview, Darcy. Why would you pass up an opportunity like this?"

"M-my stutter." Darcy clutched her coffee cup with both hands.

"Pfft. I know you've been putting together an eloquence potion." Aunt Willow stirred her tea, the spoon tinking against the ceramic. "If you need more time to make it, I can try to reschedule your tests."

"No." The words Darcy needed to say felt like a lump in the pit of her stomach. "Even if I p-pass the tests, I'll n-never meet the coven's standards."

"You may never be good at casting, but you can be an asset to the coven in other ways. Your herbs, for instance. We always need herbs, and Hazel charges an arm and a leg for her components." Willow reached across the table and put her red-tipped fingers on the back of Darcy's hand. "Witchcraft runs in your blood. Don't just ignore it. You need to be with your own kind."

The affirmation was a little backhanded, but it made Darcy feel good, nonetheless. Aunt Willow wasn't big on compliments. It gave her the courage to repeat a question she'd asked a dozen times. "Why did Mom leave the coven?"

Willow's face darkened, and she removed her hand. "None of that matters. I've let it go. The coven has put it behind them. Let it be enough that they're willing to take you back."

"You p-promised them I'm not like Mom. How can I not be like Mom if I don't even know what she did?" Darcy felt sick to her stomach. Mom hadn't talked about her early life, and the few things she'd let slip out had made Darcy believe Mom's family didn't love her. The day Darcy met her mother's sister, she'd braced herself to be snubbed. But Aunt Willow had put her arms around her and cried. She'd given seventeen-year-old Darcy a place to live and even tried to teach her spells, which Mom had refused to do.

After a moment of consideration, Aunt Willow leaned forward. "Loyalty. Integrity. Truthfulness." She pushed her chair away from the table and rose. "As long as you maintain those things, you will never be like your mother."

The lump in Darcy's throat made it difficult to speak as her aunt turned to go. Willow was the only family she had, and Darcy wanted to please her. But she also wanted to be accepted as she was, and that included Adrian. Aunt Willow had reached the café door by the time Darcy blurted out, "I met my fated mate."

Her aunt turned slowly, eyebrows drawn into a frown. "Witches don't have fated mates."

"I d-do." She pulled aside the collar of her shirt, exposing the healing mark of Adrian's claim.

Aunt Willow's face twitched in an array of emotions before she shook her head. With a sigh, she said, "Congratulations," and left.

Darcy sat for long moments, back stiff and tea growing cold. Well, what had she expected out of the encounter? Now at least Aunt Willow knew. The pressure to join the coven was off. *What do I do now?* Without someone to teach her, she may have set herself an impossible task. Maybe she should just give in and become a shifter. But much as she loved Adrian and his magnificent mountain lion, she wanted to be a witch. She had ever since she could remember. Aunt Willow was right that witchcraft ran in her blood.

She rose from the table and paid the bill, then headed outside to her Subaru with heavy footsteps. Only yesterday she'd walked this same path with Adrian, feeling light as air. She glanced down the street toward the trees where they'd made out and her gaze fell on the apothecary sign. Hazel was always nice to her. Would she consider taking Darcy as an apprentice?

Licking her lips, she turned away from her car and walked the short distance to the shop. The bell rang as she entered, and Jake looked up from his bed near the register, blinked at her, then lowered his muzzle back to his paws as if unconcerned.

Hazel called from the back, "Be right out."

Darcy wandered toward the rack of loose tea, reading off the names without really comprehending them. Her mind churned over what to say. Hazel had left her coven, and hadn't joined Aunt Willow's when she moved here. Did that mean she didn't want to associate with other witches? Then why would she run a shop that sold spell supplies? *She sells tea, too.* Darcy picked up a cellophane baggie of spruce tip tea.

When Hazel spoke from behind her, Darcy nearly jumped out of her skin. "Hi, Darcy."

Spinning to face the shop keeper, Darcy stuttered, "D-do you have any b-books on spell casting?"

Hazel's eyes seemed to sparkle, and Darcy thought she saw the ghost of a smile fleet over her lips. "Of course. You seem to have an interest in herbs. How about one on potions?"

Darcy nodded mutely.

Hazel bent and opened a cabinet below the jewelry case and removed a leather-bound book the size of her palm. She handed it to Darcy.

Darcy licked her lips and ran her fingers over the embossed flower on the front. The book looked like someone's diary rather than anything magical. Inside, tiny handwriting filled the pages. She read a few lines to herself. *Potion making basics. Herbs both grown and harvested. Choosing the right vial.*

She looked up at Hazel and smiled. "How m-much?"

"Consider it a loan." Hazel glanced toward the door and leaned forward. "The coven doesn't like these books to be shared, so don't tell anyone you have it, all right?"

Tears pricked the back of Darcy's eyes. "Why are you being so nice?"

Hazel's lips thinned and she hesitated a moment before answering. "I knew your mother. She was a lot older than me, but I remember the way the others ran her off. It isn't right for them to make you suffer for her choices."

"What did she do?" Darcy stared wide-eyed at Hazel. Maybe she'd finally get some answers after all.

Hazel sighed, "She had an affair with Willow's husband, who was also the coven leader's son. It was a huge scandal."

Shock made Darcy's breath hitch. Her mother had never talked about her father, said he'd been a one-night-stand. "W-was he my father?"

Hazel shook her head. "No, he died before you were conceived. The coven found out about the affair after he left everything to your mother."

Suddenly, Darcy understood how Mom had afforded the big house in Anchorage on her income selling jewelry. She still didn't know who her father was, and probably never would, but that didn't matter. At least she understood why Aunt Willow acted the way she did, at least a little. "Thank you for telling me."

Hazel smiled. "If you need any help with that book, let me know. Most of the spells in there require little if any incantations."

"Are you offering to teach me?"

Hazel rubbed her fingertips over her mouth, looking once more toward the door. "Your aunt will hate me for it, but yes. I'll teach you. But only if you come to work for me. I can't run this shop by myself." She winked. "And Jake's terrible at running the till."

Darcy laughed and hugged the book against her chest, her heart so full, she was certain it might burst. "Deal. Thank you."

"Now go study that while I figure out what I'm going to do with you."

Nodding, Darcy left, silently singing to herself, *I'm finally going to be a witch!*

Adrian crouched against the soft, mossy floor at the edge of the clearing and waited as tiny footsteps passed by his hiding spot for the third time. He let out a soft purr and twitched his tail against the nearby branches. The feet stopped. Over his head, leaves rustled, revealing a cherubic face with blonde curls and her mother's ice-blue eyes. His two-year-old daughter squealed in delight. "Foun' you!"

Extending his front paws out straight, Adrian arched his back in a stretch while Lu's chubby hands reached for his neck. She wrapped both arms around him and climbed onto his back as if he was a pony, giggling as he rose. This was a game she never tired of playing, and he was happy to oblige. His wanderings these days kept him close to home, close to his family. One day, his daughter might discover she had an animal, and he would show her the deeper forest. Or, like her mother, she might become a witch. Either option was beautiful to Adrian, as long as she was part of his life.

With the girl on his back, he strolled toward the cabin. Fresh laundry hung drying in the sun, and Darcy had just finished making a batch of soap for the apothecary, filling the air with fresh sandalwood and floral essences. The cabin took up more of the clearing since he'd added two more rooms, including a separate building for Darcy's herb drying and a small garden plot full of fragrant plants and flowers. She and Hazel had branched into Internet orders for the shop, and Darcy's potions and lotions—both magical and non-magical—had become a big hit with their clientele.

Lu slipped from his shoulders and went running toward the front porch. The rickety chair had been replaced with a porch swing, and she clambered onto it, the chain rattling.

He shifted back to a man and hurried up the steps to help her before she fell off and hurt herself. Darcy emerged from inside carrying a box of soaps. Her gaze slid down his body to his crotch, then she met his eyes with a lewd eyebrow wriggle. His cock swelled in response. He reached for a nearby pair of shorts to cover himself. "Damn it, woman."

She smirked and set the box down next to several others, waiting until his shorts were in place before wrapping both arms around his waist. Her eyes said I love you without her needing to speak a word.

He kissed her nose. "I love you too, even if you are going to scar our daughter for life with your effect on me."

Lu now sat on the bench swing, bumping her back against the swing ineffectually as she tried to make the seat move. "Swing!"

Letting go of his mate, Adrian sat, and Darcy took the opposite side, sandwiching Lu between them. Adrian put one arm along the backrest, kneading Darcy's shoulder lightly. She rubbed her cheek against his forearm and smiled. Together, they pushed the swing back and let it pendulum forward while their daughter laughed with joyful abandon.

EPILOGUE

Kepler sat in his office at the Trooper station and read the police report for what had to be the hundredth time, mentally grumbling about the sloppiness of the photos. *Not sloppiness, ignorance,* he reminded himself. The rookie who'd sent him the intel wasn't from his office. Hell, he wasn't even with the State Troopers, just a beat cop in Kenai. But Kepler had to give him credit for taking initiative.

Zooming in on the image on his computer, he tried to get a better look at the white streak in the victim's hair. The report didn't state that the dead woman was a shifter, but the similarity to the rogue cases he'd been investigating in the Wrangell-St. Elias area for the last three years couldn't be denied. He picked up his phone and tapped in the number Officer Cal Bennet had included in the email with the report.

A deep voice answered, "Bennett."

"Hello, this is Kepler Stone with the state's Major Crimes Unit. Is this a good time to talk?"

In the background, Kepler heard the ticking of a turn signal, then Bennet said, "Stone, I'm glad you called. My only contact down here keeps blowing me off."

"I appreciate you coming to me. I assume the victim in these photos was a shifter?"

"Yeah. A wolf. I keep an ear out for shifter crimes, and this matches the rogues in Wrangell about a year ago."

The trail Kepler'd been following had gone cold, which had been both a relief and frustration. At least no more shifters were dying in the area. But the outbreak could happen again unless they found the cause. *It has happened again.* "Tell me what you know."

Cal described the death, which had been attributed to hypothermia. "There wasn't any sign of a struggle, and as far as I know, no other shifters were involved, but you know shifters don't die of hypothermia. Plus, the crime scene smelled like ashes, and the victim's white hair was on the exact same spots as the ones in your reports. I think this case is related to yours."

"Seems likely." The most recent theory was that a witch was behind the outbreak of rogues, but the Head of Covens said she needed a fresh sample in order to determine what type of magic was being used. "This could be just the break we need. Can you get a tissue sample?"

"Body's been cremated. The family didn't want things drawn out."

"Shit." That meant this was a dead end unless another rogue turned up. The last thing he wanted was more deaths. Kepler rubbed his temple, torn between hoping Cal was mistaken and wanting another lead. "Make sure you get a sample to me if another one shows up."

"I can try, but the only way I find out about these things is through the grapevine," Cal said. "I've tried to get on the state task force, but I don't have the credentials. There are no shifters on the investigation team in the Major Crimes Unit down here."

Fuck. A shifter with jurisdiction needed to be at the scene if this happened again, and Kepler knew in his gut this wasn't the end of things. He opened Google and looked at the map of the small Alaskan town on the banks of the Kenai River. "Looks like I'm transferring to Kenai, then."

Cal said, "Great, let me know when you arrive and I'll show you around."

"Thanks." Kepler hung up the phone and began the paperwork for his transfer. Mom and Dad would be sorry to see him leave, but it was time he broke away from the Gakona pack. His wolf had been chafing under the new pack Alpha, Gray. The guy wasn't bad, but Kepler wasn't ready to swear allegiance just because his family had.

He only hoped the pack Alpha down south wasn't an asshole...

Dear Reader,

I hope you enjoyed visiting Alaska in this paranormal romance. Want to find out what is happening with the rogue shifters? The mystery continues in Kepler's book, Bewitched Shifter.

Ashlyn Reed came to Alaska to run a bakery, but after she's attacked in a dark alley and the guy ends up dead, the hot detective investigating the case tells her she's not only a werewolf, but his fated mate. Can either one be true?

Visit your favorite bookstore to get your copy now, or turn the page for a sneak peek. Thank you for reading!

XOXO,
Tamsin

. . .

P.S. Be sure to check out all the Alaska Alphas books at:
https://books2read.com/rl/aurorashifters

BEWITCHED SHIFTER EXCERPT

*M*usic from the bar shook the sidewalk under Ashlyn's feet as she waited for the bouncer to check her ID. She'd let her new hair stylist talk her into "mermaid hair," and the pink and blue color seemed to make people think she was younger than her twenty-five years. That, and the fact that she was carrying cupcakes.

"They're mojito flavored," she told the bouncer, feeling stupid. *Who brings cupcakes to a bar?* "For a bachelorette party."

"Ah." The bouncer returned her card with a wink and waved her in. "They came in a while ago. Have fun."

"Thanks." She smiled and stepped inside. Since moving to Kenai a couple of months ago to take over her cousin's bakery, she'd come to appreciate how friendly the locals were. Even this bachelorette party was proof of that. Between baking and catching up on the mess Cousin Lana had called bookkeeping, she'd barely had time to meet anyone. Muffy, a local bride-to-be, had come into the bakery looking for a quote on a wedding cake and, after learning Ashlyn was new in town, had invited her to the party.

Ashlyn wasn't usually one to take invitations from complete strangers, but she needed friends, and Muffy seemed nice. At least the party would get her out of the house.

Pausing just inside the door, she scanned the crowd for Muffy's familiar face. Multi-colored lights flashed over a tiny dance floor packed with people, and patrons hovered around high-topped tables nearby. A long bar extended through the center of the room, and the delicious aroma of fresh Alaskan halibut and steak fries drifted from the kitchen in the back. Her stomach growled. She'd been too busy for lunch today, and sugary cupcakes weren't going to cut it, especially if she was going to be drinking.

Laughter caught her attention from several semi-circular booths along the wall. A group of women in low-cut blouses held shot glasses in the air, and she spied Muffy's dark, artistically-tousled tresses beneath a sparkly plastic tiara. Nerves tightened her belly. She wasn't shy, but joining a clique of women who already knew each other was always awkward. Too bad Cousin Lana was busy on her fishing boat or Ashlyn would've made her come along.

Straightening her shoulders, she headed over, looking at Muffy's white sash proclaiming her soon-to-be hitched status. *Cliché*. But she kind of liked cliché. It felt stable. Predictable.

The bride-to-be spotted her and rose, leaning across the table and waving her manicured pink fingertips in a shooing motion at her other friends. "Scoot over, let Ashlyn in. Ashlyn, this is Jen, my sister. She's visiting from Idaho. I'm trying to convince her she should move here." She pointed to the auburn haired woman Ashlyn settled next to, then toward the other women at the table. "And these are my friends Bev, Christy, and Alison."

The women greeted her with smiles, and Ashlyn felt a warming welcome flow through her. She hadn't realized how much she missed hanging out with friends. She didn't know these ladies yet, but they seemed really nice, and the penis-themed gag gifts scattered across the table promised they had a sense of humor. *Maybe they'll even appreciate my bad jokes.* But first, she'd bribe them with cupcakes.

Ashlyn held out the pink pastry box. "I thought you might like some treats."

"Oh, you're so sweet. You shouldn't have!" Muffy set the box aside and pushed a shot glass at her. "Here, drink. You need to catch up!"

The sharp scent of tequila wafted from the glass. Last time she'd had tequila, she'd turned into a bitch and alienated everyone at the party. Not that Ryan, her ex, hadn't deserved every ounce of her alcohol-fueled anger, but she definitely could've handled the break up better. "No thanks. Really."

"Oh, come on! The bakery is closed tomorrow!" Muffy wiggled her shoulders in time to the music, gravity-defying breasts staying perfectly in place. "Live it up a little."

Ashlyn reached for the laminated menu buried beneath the gag gifts. "I haven't had dinner yet."

"We have appetizers on the way." Muffy splayed a hand over the menu, pressing it flat against the table. "Don't worry."

Jen leaned closer, auburn tresses cascading over bare shoulders. "Just do the one and she'll leave you alone."

"At least until the next time someone says you know what!" Bev—a blonde who Ashlyn thought might've been in the bakery a time or two—gave an exaggerated wink.

"What words are we not allowed to say?"

"Oh, she's sneaky!" Jen laughed. "Trying to trick us into saying them out loud."

"I told you you'd like her." Muffy leaned over to drape a string of Mardi Gras beads over Ashlyn's head. "Jen made a list. It's somewhere in there." She gestured to the baubles strewn over the table. "But everyone has to do at least one shot to start."

Ashlyn was a lightweight, and any amount of alcohol would go right to her head. On the other hand, a small buzz *would* help her relax. She tipped the shot glass back. The tequila burned an oily trail down her throat, followed by a moment of vertigo. *Whoa, that was fast.* She scrunched her eyes and shook her head. "Ack!"

"Yeah!" several of the ladies at the table cheered.

Ashlyn accepted a piece of paper titled BACHELORETTE BINGO as another round of shots arrived. The waitress set a glass in front of her and Ashlyn said, "Thank you."

That was apparently one of the things they weren't allowed to say, and the women around her started chanting, "Drink! Drink!"

Stomach twisting, Ashlyn looked over her shoulder, hoping for the promised appetizers. The waitress had moved to another table, but food had to be arriving soon, right? *You didn't come out tonight to be a party-pooper.* Taking a deep breath, she lifted the glass and downed it.

She knew right away she'd made a mistake. Stomach revolting, she shot to her feet. "Excuse me."

"Are you going to the bathroom? Wait for me," Muffy said.

Ashlyn didn't wait. The tequila was coming up, and she'd prefer not to spew all over her new friends. The bathrooms had to be near the back, right? She elbowed through the crowd of sweaty bodies to reach the rear of the bar. No bathrooms, only a door to the kitchen and an emergency exit. Tequila rising in her throat, she shoved against the exit door.

Blessedly cool night air flooded over her, and she only managed to stumble a few steps outside before she doubled over and heaved into the dirt alley. After a couple of spasms, her stomach was empty. She rested with her hands on her knees, panting. Glancing upward, she noticed the aurora borealis was out, ribbons of green light roiling behind wisps of clouds. This was the first time she'd seen the lights since moving here, and she wished she was in a better condition to enjoy them.

The alley remained quiet but for the muffled beat of the music from inside as she took a few deep breaths. Ugh, she hated throwing up. And the smell—it'd been gross out here before she'd barfed. Now it was disgusting. At least the door didn't appear to have been hooked to an alarm.

Straightening, she wiped her mouth against the back of her hand and turned to the bar. She collided into the solid chest of a man. *Fuck.* The bouncer must've come to check on her. She raised her chin. "Excuse me, I was…"

A pair of glowing purple eyes met hers.

She gasped and stumbled back. She'd heard of tequila giving people hallucinations, but she'd never had any herself.

The man opened his mouth, exposing unnaturally pointed teeth. She backed up another step. Her heart was about to pound its way out of her chest. His mop of hair had a white streak down the middle, and her mind immediately conjured images of Frankenstein's Bride.

Knowing it was a bad joke, but unable to stop herself, she murmured, "It's alive!"

In a move almost too quick to follow, he reached for her.

She screamed, trying to remember anything from the self-defense class she'd taken in high school. But that'd been almost ten years ago. Like claws, his fingertips jabbed into her arms, yanking her toward him. His face descended to her shoulder and pain seared through her.

Did he just bite me?

Agony surged through her. Pain. Anger. Fury. Her entire being seemed to explode in a shower of sparks and fur. *Fur?* Her lips curled back from her teeth.

The next thing she knew, her mouth was against his throat. The taste of iron coated her tongue.

Not iron. Blood.

What the fuck was happening? She wasn't in control. Her head twisted, jaws refusing to let go. She felt the tear of flesh and heard an awful gurgling as the man's hands pawed uselessly against her. The light in his eyes shifted to green, and she swore he whispered, "Thank you."

Then the glow faded to darkness.

*　　*　*　　*　*　*　　*　*

Kepler arrived on the scene as the nearby Orthodox church bell began chiming midnight. He climbed out of his Jeep and retrieved his forensics kit from the back. Red and blue police lights reflected off the bar's sheet metal roofing. Tourist season was nearly over, but a swarm of onlookers pressed against the police tape blocking the alley.

He pushed through the crowd, ignoring the irritated looks, and ducked under the police tape. The officer watching the line nodded as he passed.

Near the bar's dimly-lit rear exit, blood darkened the packed dirt between the dumpsters. The air stank of bad seafood, vomit, and garbage. Kepler forced his shifter senses down, breathing shallowly as he took in the scene. A lanky man with curly hair sprawled on his back near the rear exit, throat torn open like a package of hamburger.

Kepler paused next to a bloody paw print the size of a melon. Bear attacks weren't unheard of in the town on the banks of a river known for its salmon runs, but this wasn't the print of a bear. It was a wolf, and a big one. *A shifter*. He knew that even without verifying the scent.

Near the bar's back door, Cal, the local police officer, broke from conversation with a State Trooper and strode over, broad freckled face unusually grim. Cal was also a wolf shifter, and had been the one who'd contacted Kepler when the rogue outbreak showed up in Alaska. Both outsiders to the local pack, they'd become fast friends in the three months since Kepler'd transferred here.

Cal pulled a tube of vapor rub from the breast pocket of his police uniform and offered it to Kepler, speaking in a low voice. "Victim's a shifter. And he has those freaky white marks we've been looking for."

Kepler shook his head, declining the vapor rub. Much as he hated the scent of a crime scene, his nose often detected clues that might otherwise be overlooked. It helped him excel at his job, and he'd already earned grudging respect within the good ol' boys club that dominated the Major Crimes Unit. He bent to get a closer look at the body. "Any idea who took him out?"

"Nope." Cal shrugged. "We're telling the press it was probably a bear attack. You think you can bring me in on this one?" Cal wanted to join the forensics unit, but lacked formal training, and Kepler didn't yet have the clout to get him a position with the human-dominated state law enforcement agency.

"I'll take it up with Finch, but you know how it is. We have to maintain jurisdiction. How's class going?" Kepler'd helped him sign up for an online course.

"I fucking hate homework," Cal complained." Are you sure there isn't a way to test out?"

"The test won't use your shifter senses, Cal, you know

that. It's all about chain of custody procedures, documentation—"

"Yeah, yeah, I know." Cal waved off the familiar lecture. "I've been studying. Go do your thing. I'll keep the humans occupied. Just let me know how I can help."

Nodding, Kepler pulled out his camera and started taking photos. The white streak definitely indicated the man had gone rogue, which meant that whoever had killed him was of secondary concern, at least to the shifter community. What or who was causing shifters to turn rogue was Kepler's primary mission. Back in Diablo Falls, the rogue outbreak had been blamed on a witch's hex, although that hadn't been proven before the outbreak ended. Steeling himself for an onslaught of sensory input, Kepler dragged in a breath, sniffing for clues. Blood. Garbage. Wolf shifter. *Mate.*

He shot to his feet and backed away. *Mate?* Not the dead shifter, but the other wolf who'd been here. The one who'd most likely made the kill. Wildflower honey and musk. A scent that made his inner wolf come to attention and demand action.

He realized he was panting when Cal offered the vapor rub again. "Change your mind?"

"I'm fine." Kepler rubbed his palms against the front of his slacks uncomfortably. All shifters longed to find their perfect match, their destined mate, but this situation was about the least romantic he could've imagined. He didn't have time to deal with a mate, especially not one who was also a suspect. "You don't smell anything unusual, right?"

"No, why?"

The back door to the bar swung open and a young woman wearing a plastic tiara emerged, phone in hand. Cal turned, one hand up to stop her. "Hey, you can't be out here."

The woman looked at the body with wide eyes. "My friend is missing and I'm worried about her."

"Well, she's not out here." Cal hurried over and ushered the woman inside.

Kepler turned back to the crime scene, gaze following the bloody paw prints circling the body. They led toward the other end of the alley. His wolf was urging him forward. Yearning to meet this woman. His human mind kept a tight leash on the beast inside him. He couldn't let hormones cloud his investigation of the crime scene.

Heart thundering against his ribs, he walked down the alley, watching every footstep to be sure he wasn't missing any clues. The prints faded quickly, but the scent of honey and female grew stronger.

He froze at the corner of a dumpster, nostrils twitching. She was here. *Right here*. His hormones were screaming at him. He called softly, "Hello?"

From inside the dumpster came a soft, breathy sob.

Throat tight, he cracked open the lid. A pair of glowing blue eyes met his…

Get Bewitched Shifter now!

ACKNOWLEDGMENTS

I couldn't have done this without my awesome critique group. Your honesty and constructive input made this book shine. Brooke, Molly, Kellie, and Louise, you are the best.

I also want to thank Kara Lockharte for supporting me when I faced a difficult decision. You helped more than you know.

Thank you Boone and Tielle for joining me on this wild adventure into Alaska Alphas. May we write many, many hot, humorous, exciting books together.

And finally, thank you to my husband and daughter for their consistent support of my long hours at the computer. I know you've felt neglected, and I will try to be better.

MORE ALASKA ALPHAS

These books all stand alone and can be read in any order.
Enjoy!

FREE ORIGIN STORY!

Alpha Origins

BY TAMSIN LEY

Untamed Instinct

Bewitched Shifter

Midnight Heat

Wild Child

BY TIELLE ST. CLARE

Twisted Shifter

Midnight Son

Too Wild to Mate

BY BOONE BRUX

Polar Shift

Midnight Storm

ABOUT THE AUTHOR

Once upon a time I thought I wanted to be a biomedical engineer, but experimenting on lab rats doesn't always lead to happy endings. Now I blend my nerdy infatuation of science with character-driven romance and guaranteed happily-ever-afters. My monsters always find their mates, with feisty heroines, tortured heroes, and all the steamy trouble they can handle. I promise my stories will never leave you hanging (although you may still crave more!)

When I'm not writing, I'll be in the garden or the kitchen, exploring Alaska with my husband, or preparing for the zombie apocalypse. I also enjoy crocheting while binge watching Netflix, playing video games, and enjoying family time during our weekly D&D session.

Interested in more about me? Join my VIP Club and get free books, notices, and other cool stuff!

www.tamsinley.com

ABOUT AURORA SHIFTERS

Aurora Shifters is a collaboration of Alaskan authors who decided to put our own Arctic spin on hot paranormal shapeshifters.

Tielle St. Clare moved to Alaska when she was seven years old and believes romances should be hot and sexy with a great story and fun characters. Learn more about her at www.tiellestclare.blogspot.com

Tamsin Ley was born and raised in Alaska and writes steamy sci-fi with a pinch of pixie dust. Find out more about her plus see pictures of her glacier trips and life in Alaska at www.tamsinley.com

Boone Brux has lived all over the world, finally settling in the icy region of Alaska. No person or escapade is off limits when it comes to weaving real life experiences into her books. Learn more at www.boonebrux.com

Be sure to join the Alaska Alphas Facebook Group! www.facebook.com/groups/alaskaalphas/

facebook.com/AlaskaAlphas

bookbub.com/authors/aurora-shifters

amazon.com/author/aurorashifters

www.ingramcontent.com/pod-product-compliance
Lightning Source LLC
Chambersburg PA
CBHW032029180726
48284CB00008B/2529